Girl in a White Hat

by

REBECCA STRATTON

Harlequin Books

TORONTO • LONDON • NEW YORK • AMSTERDAM • SYDNEY • WINNIPEG

Original hardcover edition published in 1977
by Mills & Boon Limited

ISBN 0-373-02078-3

Harlequin edition published June 1977

Printed in U.S.A.

CHAPTER ONE

CHARLOTTE liked living in Spain. She had made up her mind on that in the first few days, and it was now close on two months since she arrived. So far she had seen little more of the country than the village of San Cristóbal where she lived and worked, but she had seen nothing so far that would make her change her mind.

San Cristóbal was a straggling collection of little white houses sprawled like a scribble of chalk across the hills near the delightful Andalucían town of Arcos de la Frontera, and set against a background of dark green orange groves and lighter green olive groves. Chequered over the artificially fertile countryside, they looked like a giant chessboard, with silver ribbons of precious water carried by an ancient irrigation system from the cooler hills, glinting in the hot bright sun.

The olive trees with their grey twisted trunks spread like huge spiders' webs below their dusky foliage, while the oranges groves scented the whole countryside, their heady sweet perfume hanging in the hot shimmering air like an incense that was sometimes almost overpowering in its sweetness.

Charlotte had visited Arcos a couple of times and quite enjoyed the change for an hour or so, but she found a kind of lazy tranquillity in San Cristóbal that was infinitely satisfying, and she was for the most part utterly content with her lot. Indeed she counted herself very lucky to be there, for a series of happy coincidences had led to her coming, and she had still to shake herself sometimes to make sure she was not dreaming it all.

It seemed almost unbelievable that it was only a little over three months since Charlotte's mother had bumped into an old school friend while she was shopping in the Surrey town where they lived, someone she had known before the other woman went to university where she met and married a fellow student who came from Spain. Their studies complete, the couple had gone to live in his country and the two school friends had never met since—until that day.

It was not long before they got into conversation about the old days, and an invitation to tea the following day had led to the first meeting between Charlotte and her mother's friend, Martha Berganza. She explained that she was in England mostly for a holiday with her family, but that she also had in mind the idea of taking back with her an English girl as secretary-companion.

Since the death of her husband, four years previously, she had been rather lonely. Her son was at university, or had been until recently, and she was also, she confessed, a little homesick for an English voice sometimes. Giving up her house in Spain to return to England was unthinkable, she said, because for one thing Spain had now become her home, but taking an English girl into her employ seemed an ideal solution.

When she heard about it, Charlotte could hardly believe such a coincidence. She had spent three years at secretarial college after leaving school, followed by a further three years in a rather dull but well paid job with an industrial firm, and for some time she had been on the lookout for something more interesting. The

6

idea of becoming a secretary-companion to her mother's old school friend, and of living in Spain, appealed to her enormously, and Martha Berganza had been equally anxious that she should take the job.

They had taken to one another right away and there were no character differences that were likely to make things difficult in the future, so that accepting seemed to be the answer to both their needs. Martha in fact treated her more like a daughter than an employee, and insisted on being called Aunt Martha in preference to Mrs Berganza. The initial wrench of leaving her family and her home had soon been overcome by the excitement of a new country, and she had adapted to the different environment so quickly and easily that she had even surprised herself.

Martha's only child, her son Luis, was a couple of years older than Charlotte and as swarthily handsome as his father had been when Martha married him. He had done well at university and had only recently qualified as a lawyer, but was not yet practising, a fact that seemed sometimes to worry his mother, who on more than one occasion had remarked that he should find himself a wife and then perhaps he would settle down to work.

Lately, in fact, Charlotte had been left in little doubt that Martha Berganza saw a match between her son and her old friend's pretty daughter as an ideal solution, although she had received no encouragement from the two young people. In the meantime Charlotte continued to enjoy Luis's company without committing herself to anything more serious than the occasional drive out to go sightseeing. She was still only twenty-three and there was plenty of time to think about settling down.

Some of the roads in rural Andalucía left a great deal to be desired, being both badly surfaced and very dusty, and the narrow track that served San Cristóbal was probably among the worst. Few of the inhabitants bothered to complain, however, and there was no one else to do so. Virtually no cars passed through the village, for it was off the recognised tourist routes, and there were only two homes in San Cristóbal wealthy enough to own vehicles.

Through her fairly frequent visits to the post office and the village shop, Charlotte had become accustomed to the tortuous dusty road with its potholed surface, and it scarcely bothered her. Just as she had become quite adept at taking the sudden sharp turn at the bottom of the hill that led into the village proper, without losing her balance or hitting anything.

Her English-made bicycle was the only such vehicle in San Cristóbal, and had at first been an object of great interest. By now the village people were quite accustomed to seeing her spinning along, with her long blonde hair streaming out behind her and her light cotton dresses revealing perhaps rather more of her slim tanned legs than would normally have been acceptable.

She still attracted a certain amount of interest whenever she made her excursions to the village, but on the whole she was now an accepted part of their community. They accepted her foreignness with the customary tolerance of Spanish hospitality, and smiled at the sight of the pretty English girl as she made her way to Señora Blanco's little *tienda*.

Today she wore a pale blue dress that complemented her pale gold tan and added depth to her blue eyes, and her corn-gold hair was, as always, crowned by a small lacy-brimmed hat that shaded her eyes and kept the worst of the heat from her head and neck.

As usual the people she passed on her way called out a friendly *'Buenas tardes, señorita!'* and waved a hand, while at the same time shaking their heads slowly, as if they were telling themselves that they really should disapprove of such rash behaviour on the part of a young woman. Those who might have considered her indecorous, however, were charmed from disapproval by the wide, dazzling smile and the frankness of her blue eyes.

Possibly few people understood Charlotte's exact position in the Berganza household, but that was the concern of Señora Berganza, and she was well known enough and popular enough to be considered incapable of housing a young woman who was other than respectable. The fact that the golden-haired English girl was seen about with the Señora's eligible son was perhaps significant, but that too was the concern of the Señora.

Probably because her mind was less on what she was doing than on other things as she took the corner at the bottom of the hill, the action of turning was more automatic than conscious. There was seldom need to look out for traffic, and she had done the same trip so often during the past couple of months that she automatically cut in close without slowing down.

It was therefore all the more startling when she found herself on a collision course as she sped the last few metres down into the village, and although she applied her brakes in desperate haste she was not quite quick enough. She hastily recalled the Spanish word of warning and called out as she clung on grimly.

It was fortunate, for him at least, that the man she

collided with was a tall and unyielding obstacle and instead of being knocked over by the collision he stood firm. In a swift cool reaction that was startling in its suddenness, he caught the handlebars of her bicycle as she brushed against him and swung the machine round and away from him, with Charlotte still in the saddle.

She gained no more than a fleeting impression of dark eyes that glittered with either anger or surprise, and a pair of strong brown hands that swung her from her path, before she landed with undignified force at the side of the road. The breath was knocked out of her and she lay more or less at the stranger's feet.

There she lay for a moment, too stunned to realise exactly what had happened to her. Her dress had been rucked up as she fell and showed most of her slim legs, while her hat lay some distance away in the dust of the road. It was while she shook herself back to realisation and hastily pulled down her dress, that a shadow fell across her, a long dark shadow that blocked out the warmth of the sun and made her glance up quickly to seek the cause of it.

The man who stood over her seemed much too reminiscent of a figure of vengance for comfort, and there was an aura of raw emotion about him that tangled with her own confused reactions and made her shudder. Possibly her blonde hair gave him a clue, or perhaps he knew who she was, for he addressed her in English, his voice hard and disapproving, despite a vibrance that betrayed the passion of anger barely suppressed.

'You have little regard, it seems, *señorita*, either for your own safety or that of others!'

His English was impeccable; precise and pedantic but faultless, and for some reason she found that surprising. Charlotte knew who he was, for she had seen him once or twice before; only then he had been driving a sleek and expensive sports car, and Luis had spoken of him as if he held him in some awe. In the village of San Cristóbal she could hardly have chosen a worse victim for her carelessness.

She scrambled to her feet, rather surprisingly assisted by a hard strong hand that gripped her arm with more impatience than anxiety to help, she feared, and for the first time she looked in to his face. Luis had named him as Don Gerardo Cortez, the latest in a long and ancient line, and seeing him close to for the first time Charlotte admitted to being curious enough to make a hurried and surreptitious survey of him while she apologised.

He was very tall and very dark, and the strong uncompromising features confirmed the Moorish ancestry that the Cortez were reputed to be proud of. The Moorish conquerers who had held sway in Spain for several hundred years and still left the mark of their strong hawkish features on their present-day descendants.

An impressive man, and one to be reckoned with if Luis's opinion was to be taken seriously. The Cortez family had once been powerful as well as wealthy and they had owned the whole of San Cristóbal as well as much more beside. The influence of the Cortez name in the village still carried weight and its present bearer still lived in the huge rugged castle that dominated the countryside, perched like a glowering eagle on its towering rock foundation. He was not an easy man to apologise to.

'I'm very sorry, *señor*.' She hesitated to use his name, since Spanish manners were more inclined to be strictly formal, and they had never been formally introduced, although she was convinced he knew her identity as well as she knew his. 'I—I hope I didn't hurt you.'

The brief glimpse of humour that she caught in his dark eyes, for only a second or two, both surprised and startled her. 'Any hurt is much more likely to be to yourself, *señorita*, than to me—you are not hurt?'

'Oh no—thank you!' She laughed reflectively as she brushed down the pale blue dress with hands that were alarmingly unsteady after the fall. 'My dignity has suffered, but nothing else.'

'I wished to avoid a collision and my reaction was instinctive.' It was not an apology, nor did it suggest that there might have been an alternative method of avoiding the collision, but it had been her fault and she could not complain.

She recalled that split-second reaction, the swift graceful turn of the lean body, like that of a dancer as he swung her clear. 'You pivoted like a matador!' She had no real idea why she chose the simile, for she knew little about the *corrida*, except that she disliked it, and Gerardo Cortez looked at her for a second, his eyes slightly narrowed, rather as if he found the remark suspect.

'You are familiar with the fact that I have fought in the *corrida*, *señorita*?'

Even the thought of it repelled her, but she did her best not to let her opinion show, for the Spanish, she knew, could be touchy on the subject of their national sport. Instead she breathed a rather exaggerated sigh of relief and chose to ignore the invitation to comment.

'Well, I'm thankful no one was hurt!'

She could not understand why he did not simply end the episode there and then. It was out of character for a man of his breeding to be standing there with her, even if she had almost knocked him down. It would have been more in keeping, more usual, for him to have simply inquired if she was unharmed, bowed politely and gone on his way, and his departure from convention puzzled as well as intrigued her.

The dark eyes regarded her for a moment before he spoke, and she wondered why she felt so small and insignificant suddenly. 'You could quite easily have been killed, had you arrived a moment later,' he told her, and indicated the big black sports car that stood in the shade just a short distance away. 'Another moment and I would have been driving, *señorita*, not walking, and the consequence would have been rather less happy for you.'

Glancing at the big gleaming car, Charlotte shivered. What he said was true; a moment later taking that corner she would have been in collision with a moving car instead of with a man on foot, and for the first time she realised just how close she had come to disaster. Looking up at him, she ventured some kind of explanation, however ineffectual.

'I hadn't realised,' she confessed. 'I suppose it's a classic case of familiarity breeds contempt.' She wondered if he was familiar with the proverb, despite his excellent command of English, for he frowned briefly before he replied.

'A dangerous truth, *señorita*, especially in such circumstances.' He glanced at her uncovered head, at the shining gold hair that was slightly dishevelled after her fall, then he walked the short distance to where her hat lay on the dusty road and retrieved it, brushing the dust from it with a large hand before he handed it to her. 'Too much Andalucían sun is also dangerous when

13

one is not a native to it—your hat, *señorita*.'

'Thank you.' Charlotte replaced the little white hat on her head, then looked up at him once more. She still could not understand why he was defying convention to stand and talk with her, but she was sufficiently intrigued by him not to mind the delay. 'I count myself almost a native now,' she told him with a smile. 'I've been here almost two months now.'

'Not yet long enough to consider yourself immune from *la insolación*, I think, *señorita*.' Once more his gaze was directed at her head where the little white hat now covered the crown of her head at least. 'That is no doubt why you always wear that hat, is it not?'

It took Charlotte a second or two to realise the significance of the remark, but when she did it gave her a curious feeling in the pit of her stomach, for it seemed to suggest that he had observed her rather more often than she had realised. Her laugh was a little unsteady, and her thick lashes concealed the expression in her eyes.

'You seem quite well informed, Señor Cortez,' she said, and a raised brow remarked briefly on her use of his name.

'As do you, *señorita*—you have the advantage of me!'

It was difficult for Charlotte to believe he was unfamiliar with her name when he knew everything that went on in the village, according to Luis. Something of the feudal power of his ancestors still remained, though it could be no more than a frail ghost of that possessed by his forebears, and he would surely know the name of the newest addition to Señora Berganza's household, especially since she was a foreigner and therefore of special interest.

Despite her certainty, however, she told him her name though her blue eyes challenged his professed ignorance. 'I'm Charlotte Grey,' she told him. 'I work for Mrs—Señora Berganza; but you know that, of course.'

The jibe was irresistible, but she saw the wide firm mouth tighten for a moment as if he resented it, then he took her proffered hand in his own strong hard fingers and held it just a fraction longer than was necessary. '*Sí*, I knew that, *señorita*.' The dark, depthless eyes made her hold their steady gaze for a moment. 'It displeases you?'

Charlotte felt suddenly as if things were going a little too fast from her, and she shook her head almost without realising it. 'I—I can hardly be surprised that you know what's going on in your own village,' she said. Across the road a couple of women gossiped together beside the rough stone cross that marked the centre of the village, and she could almost feel their interest; sense the curious, flicking glances in her direction. 'I hope you'll excuse me, *señor*, I really ought to go— I'm on an errand for Señora Berganza.'

'*Sin duda, señorita*.' He inclined his head in a stiffly formal bow, as if he too had become aware of those interested eyes across the tiny square. 'I trust that when we meet again it will be in less dangerous circumstances.'

The assumption that they would meet again rather surprised Charlotte, though she tried not to let it show when she nodded and smiled. Luis had implied that, while he was kept abreast of matters in the village, Don Gerardo in fact seldom had contact with anyone in San Cristóbal. Remarking that he probably found his pleasures elsewhere, Luis had left her in little doubt of his meaning, something she had no difficulty in believing now that she had met the man.

'At least I shall take more care when I come round that corner next time!' she assured him.

Bending down, he retrieved her bicycle from the road and gave it a swift and cursory examination before handing it over. Then once more he made that small and very formal bow, bold black eyes holding her gaze steadily. '*Buenas tardes*, Señorita Grey!'

Charlotte watched him, as he strode across to the parked car, with a slightly dazed look in her blue eyes, and hastily brought herself back to earth when he started the engine. It roared into life, shattering the hot dusty stillness of the village square, then pulled away and swooped past Charlotte as she stood at the roadside.

She caught a fleeting glimpse of a long brown hand raised in a mock salute, an even more brief impression of white teeth in the dark features, and he was gone. By the stone cross the two women, made bolder by his departure, watched her for a moment until she moved towards them, heading for the little shop. It was something fresh for them to gossip about, she thought wrly—Señora Berganza's visitor chatting in public with Don Gerardo.

It sometimes surprised Charlotte to realise just how quickly she had become accustomed to living in such very different surroundings. Martha Berganza's home was completely Spanish despite the English origins of its mistress, and yet she felt at home there even after only a few weeks. It was no hardship, of course, living in such a lovely place, for the Berganza home lacked nothing in the way of comforts.

Her own room, for instance, overlooked the country-side beyond the gardens; the patterns of light and dark green of olive and orange groves that sprawled across the plains below the hills, and the glimpse between surrounding trees of the huge and rather grim looking castle on the rock that was the home of the man she had met in the village only that afternoon.

Castillo Cortez was a landmark for miles around, and it was difficult to overlook. In fact it was probably for this reason that it had been built where it was, where the people who were ruled from it could see and be constantly reminded of their overlord and his power of life and death over them. She had no idea what the inside of the castle looked like, but it was almost certainly not as comfortable or as homely as her present surroundings.

A large antique bed occupied pride of place, draped in thick Spanish lace and placed where the occupant had a breathtaking view through the window across the Andalucían landscape. The high curved window had green shutters that kept the heat of the sun at bay yet still admitted a cool breeze from the hills and the scents of roses and magnolias from the gardens below.

The soft sound of a fountain had a soothing and cooling effect too, and added one more embellishment to an already exotic and beautiful setting. Ancient brass lamps and a huge polished black wood chest nearly three hundred years old and beautifully carved and gilded, soft carpets underfoot and her own private bathroom, were added luxuries that made her feel she was more in the position of an honoured guest than an employee.

Sometimes, and more especially lately, she had in-

17

deed begun to wonder whether Martha Berganza's main objective in employing her was to bring her son into contact with a girl of her own nationality in the hope of acquiring an English daughter-in-law, for she did everything possible to encourage their being together.

As she left her room to go down to dinner, Charlotte mused on what Martha's reaction was likely to be to her recent encounter with Don Gerardo Cortez. As far as she knew her employer had no social contact with her distinguished neighbour, but then, according to Luis, few people in the district did.

The idea of someone still living in feudal isolation and splendour in that huge fortress-like castle had been intriguing enough before, but now that she had actually met the man himself, she found the idea even more intriguing. If she could do it without arousing too much comment, she would like to discover something more about both the man and his way of life. Feudalism was virtually dead in England, but she suspected it might be less so in Spain, at least in the case of Don Gerardo Cortez and the village of San Cristóbal.

Luis was already downstairs when she came into the big cool *comedor* with its long table already laid for dinner, and he turned and smiled, as he always did when he first caught sight of her. His courtesy was unfailing, and as charming as his looks.

He was handsome. Not ruggedly autocratic as Gerardo Cortez was, but possessed of fine clear-cut features and dark hair that curled slightly, and bright dark eyes that stressed every compliment he paid her, and said so much more than mere words could on occasion.

He was of average height, but still seemed tall beside Charlotte's petite build, and his skin had a light golden look that was much lighter than the usual Andaluz, thanks to his English mother. He was very attractive and very handsome and he was fully aware of both factors—but that too was in some curious way part of his charm. He had a naïve kind of conceit that was irresistible, and she smiled as she came across the room to join him.

He reached out a hand when she came within touching distance. 'Charlotte!'

With Luis, every meeting was an occasion and sometimes, with her English sense of the ridiculous, Charlotte felt the urge to giggle uncontrollably when he indulged his Spanish tendency to dramatise. Always, though, she managed to react appropriately, for to have laughed would have been unthinkable in response to a very real compliment, and she would not have hurt him or insulted him for anything. She liked him far too much for that, though not in the way his mother perhaps hoped for.

'Hello, Luis.' She let him take her hand and was quite accustomed now to the slight squeeze he gave her fingers. 'I wondered if I was late.'

He shook his head reassuringly. 'Mamá is not down yet, there's plenty of time.'

His speech was usually normal cultured English when he was in her company, and he had no accent at all to speak of, no more than a slight and charming pedantry. It was only when he felt really deeply about something and failed to find sufficient satisfaction in the more prosaic English that he resorted to his native tongue. If he was driven to using oaths, they were invariably Spanish ones.

He offered her a drink when she joined him which she refused with a shake of her head. It was a ritual that they followed most evenings before dinner and which would probably continue until one time when she felt inclined to accept. He was too polite to omit the offer, even though he was certain she would refuse.

As she often did, she strolled over to the window to look out into the gardens, quiet and still in the evening light and scented with a dozen different scents from the flowers and trees that grew in every available inch. The garden always gave her a feeling of peace and all-right-with-the-world and she sighed softly as she enjoyed the tranquillity of it.

'You have had a happy day?'

The phrase pleased her, and she nodded without turning round. 'I think so,' she said. 'Although I had a slight mishap this afternoon.' She spoke over her shoulder and a hint of laughter in her voice made light of the episode. 'I almost—mowed down, I suppose you could say, your local lord and master.'

She could imagine Luis's reaction as he sought her meaning, and she was not really surprised when he appeared at her side, one dark brow arched curiously. 'And who might my lord and master be?' he asked, obviously not following her meaning at all.

It was possible he would take exception to her designation of Don Gerardo as his superior, she realised as she hesitated. Despite having an English mother and his fluency in the language, Luis was very Spanish and as proud as most of his race. Charlotte smiled at him, shaking her head to deny she was serious.

'I almost ran down Don Gerardo, that's all.'

'That is all?' His eyes held disbelief as well as curiosity, and he leaned against the deep frame of the high curved window while he regarded her for a moment as if he was trying to make up his mind if she was joking or not. The English sense of humour was something that could on occasion confuse him. 'You are serious about this, Charlotte?'

'I did *nearly* run him down.' She laughed and shook her head. 'But it wasn't as bad as it sounds—I was on my bike and I took the corner into the village like I always do——'

'Too fast and too close!' Luis interjected, and she pulled a face that admitted it.

'As you say,' she allowed. 'Anyway, Don Gerardo was crossing the road and I barged more or less straight into him.'

'*Madre de Dios!*' He stared at her for a moment, then shook his head, impatient to hear the rest. 'What happened, Charlotte? Don't leave me in suspense!'

She hesitated for a second, wondering how he would react to the idea of Don Gerardo spending his time talking to her in the public square. 'First of all, I didn't quite hit him because he grabbed the bike and swung it to one side before the collision actually happened, then, with me still on it, he dumped it in the gutter.'

A sudden flush coloured Luis's handsome face and he scowled, his black brows drawn close. 'He dared to——' He bit back the words and instead continued to scowl for several seconds while he took stock of the report. 'Do you mean to tell me that he—he threw you to the ground, Charlotte? That he simply dumped you?'

It was always so difficult to judge his moods and reactions, she found. He might display remarkable coolness in response to some things, yet on occasion, as now, his passionate anger was purely Spanish and she was not yet familiar enough with the emotion to feel able to cope with it, therefore she hastened to explain.

'It was entirely my own fault,' she assured him, stressing her own casual acceptance of the fact. 'I wasn't looking where I was going, and he simply reacted instinctively and grabbed the bike as he swung round.' She remembered Don Gerardo's explanation of the reaction, and frowned curiously at Luis. 'I didn't realise he was a bullfighter,' she said.

It was plain from his expression that Luis found it hard to believe that piece of information had been imparted during the incident she was describing, and his eyes narrowed slightly, she thought, as he regarded her. 'Did he tell you so?' he asked.

'Only when I raised the matter. After he—swung me round the way he did, I remarked that he had pivoted like a matador, you know the way they turn from the waist. It was just something that came into my head,' she explained hastily, 'I don't know why. The way he moved, I suppose, it reminded me of the matadors. I don't like the bullfight, but I have to admit there's an incredible grace in the way the men perform all those moves.'

'And you saw this—grace in Don Gerardo Cortez?'

There was something in his voice that struck Charlotte quite forcibly, and it took a second or two for her to realise that it was a new and disturbing aspect of Luis—it suggested he might be jealous of her opinion of the other man, and she did not want that to happen.

'I said it struck me that he had looked like a matador,' she told him. 'And he asked how I knew he had fought in the *corrida*.' Once more she frowned at him curiously. 'Does he, Luis? Fight bulls, I mean—is he a matador?'

'He has fought as an amateur only.' It was obvious he imparted the information reluctantly. 'He hasn't been in the ring for several years now, of course. He is close on thirty-five and he was badly gored the last time out, so it's been said.'

'Oh, I see.' She felt a strange shiver of revulsion at the thought of that hard lean body being ripped by the horns of a bull, and yet in normal circumstances she would have applauded the very idea of the customary victim taking revenge. 'He looks a pretty tough specimen to me, I suppose he'd take on anything with an element of danger to it.'

Luis said nothing for a moment. He held his glass in one hand while he regarded her with deep and speculative dark eyes that did not like her interest in Don Gerardo Cortez at all, and made no secret of the fact. 'I should like to hear about this—accident,' he told her. 'Were you hurt?' He scanned her small rounded shape with frank appreciation, and shook his head. 'I see no sign of damage.'

'There isn't any,' Charlotte assured him. 'I simply landed at the side of the road, but the fall was so slight that I wasn't even grazed, and he helped me up right away. After that we introduced ourselves and exchanged a few words—of wisdom on his side and apology on mine.'

'He apologised also?'

She was unsure whether or not he expected her to confirm it, but she shook her head. 'Not exactly,' she denied. 'But he did explain that his action was instinctive, and I believed him. Besides,' she smiled ruefully, 'I couldn't blame him; it was my own fault and as he pointed out, another second or two and he would have been driving that fast car of his, then the result would have been very much more serious.'

'You take too many chances, Charlotte, I wish you wouldn't.'

His concern was touching and she appreciated it, but she did not want to take it too seriously. There was that discomforting air about him that made her uneasy and her heart was beating just slightly harder than usual as he stood beside her.

'I hadn't realised quite how many until Don Gerardo pointed it out to me,' she confessed. 'I *shall* have to watch my step when I'm turning that corner in future.'

'If it means you bumping into Don Gerardo, you will certainly have to watch your step!' Luis retorted swiftly, and before Charlotte could question his exact meaning she heard Martha Berganza coming through the hall to join them, and she shrugged lightly.

'I will,' she promised.

CHAPTER TWO

LOOKING from her bedroom window the following morning before she went down to breakfast, Charlotte pondered once more on the good fortune that had led to her mother meeting an old school friend. That chance encounter had led to so much that was exciting and different for her. The countryside of Andalucía could scarcely have been more unlike her native Surrey, but she found it fascinating and she had known very few moments of homesickness since her arrival.

Inland the country had the same bright dazzling character that had earned another part of Spain's coast its title of Costa de la Luz, Coast of Light, and she could not imagine it as ever being other than bathed in endless sunshine. It was almost too scorchingly hot for her sometimes, but she had no regrets at all about coming and she had never given a thought to returning home in the foreseeable future.

The Spanish character as well as the countryside fascinated her. Something about the people and their way of life had a suggestion of timelessness, a feeling of history that she had never been quite so strongly aware of elsewhere. It was almost automatic, as she stood there by the window, to glance across the patterned green acres of groves to the looming mass of Castillo Cortez, glowering over the surrounding countryside from its craggy bastion of tawny rock.

From the castle to its present incumbent was a natural progression of thought, and she was reminded again of the man she had so nearly collided with yesterday in the village square. Physically the memory of him was a little vague. She retained an impression of darkness and of strong autocratic features, but mainly it was the character of the man that had made the strongest impression.

The stunning impact of raw emotion when they came into contact for those few seconds, and the sensation of being almost overwhelmed by a personality that was so much stronger and more forceful than her own, remained with her long after they had gone their separate ways.

Men like Don Gerardo Cortez, she felt sure, had set out on voyages of discovery to the New World from places that were no more than a car ride away from where she was now. Strong dark swashbuckling *conquistadores* to whom danger and excitement were one and the same. She was rather startled to find her imagination running away with her and hastily shook herself back to reality—somehow she found that brief encounter with Don Gerardo Cortez very hard to forget.

As she made her way downstairs she determinedly kept her mind on what she had to do that day and, yet again, appreciated the homely grandeur of Casa Berganza. The big hall with its cool tiled floor and arched ceiling was much grander than anything she had known at home, and yet it had a cosy, friendly feeling.

Paintings lined its walls and a bronze bust of some past Berganza occupied pride of place against the longest wall and below an ancient gilt-framed mirror. He was an ancestor of Luis's who had been honoured by his country for services rendered, though Charlotte never knew just what they were.

Against another wall a huge alabaster jug held roses of every colour, gathered from the gardens, and the scent filled the hall, making her wrinkle her nose appreciatively as she crossed to the table they stood on and bent over for a moment to smell them. Their soft petals touched her cheek lightly as she bent her head, and she closed her eyes in a moment of pleasure at their coolness. Roses always seemed to her to be so English, and yet there were far more of them in the gardens here than had been in her own garden at home.

'Good morning, Charlotte!'

Recognising the voice, she straightened up and smiled. Luis looked gleamingly handsome as he came across from the stairway, and she felt a momentary flutter of response in her heartbeat when he came to join her. It would be easy enough to fall in love with him, she knew, and there was no doubt that Martha

Berganza would be delighted if it happened.

About Luis's reaction she was less sure. He was attentive and gallant, and she sometimes thought he would like to take their relationship a step further, but there were times when she wondered if he was perfectly content to leave matters as they were. Since she was equally undecided about her own feelings, she preferred to leave things as they were at the moment, and not think about Luis or anyone else in a serious vein.

He looked very spruce and more formal than usual in a dark suit and tie and a white shirt, so that she wondered if something was in the air. 'You're very businesslike this morning,' she told him, and he pulled a face.

Reaching out, he took her hand and squeezed her fingers as he always did, before letting them go again. 'I have an appointment at ten o'clock to see a friend of my father's who has promised Mamá to set me upon the road to respectability by making me a fully fledged lawyer!'

'You're going for an interview? Oh, Luis, that's wonderful—Aunt Martha will be pleased!'

He contorted his handsome features into another gloomy expression as he walked beside her, and she needed no telling that whatever feelings his mother might have about the prospect of his finding a place at last, Luis himself was not over-enthusiastic about the idea.

'I have no doubt,' he agreed. 'But Mamá does not face the prospect of sitting in a dull, gloomy office all day long. I do, and I don't relish the idea, Charlotte.'

She should treat the matter seriously, she thought, but somehow the sight of Luis's determinedly gloomy face inspired her to laughter rather than sympathy, and she looked up at him and smiled. 'But you trained all that time at university,' she reminded him, 'it would be an awful waste if you didn't make use of it, Luis.'

'I suppose so.' He made the admission grudgingly, and reached for her hand again, looking down at her with his soulful dark eyes as they went in to join his mother for breakfast. 'But I would so much rather spend the time with you, Charlotte, you surely know that is so.'

It was the first time he had made any definite suggestion about his feeling for her, and she felt her heart skip uneasily as she glanced at Martha Berganza sitting at the table. Taking note of the way her son's hand held Charlotte's tightly, Charlotte knew, and the way he bent his head very slightly to speak to her as they walked across the big bright room together.

'I have to earn my living too,' she reminded him, determinedly keeping the matter on a lighthearted level. 'I don't do nearly enough as it is for the salary Aunt Martha pays me.'

Luis murmured something in Spanish which she neither recognised nor heard quite properly, but she felt sure it was something regarding her position there. He saw her seated at the table, then went and kissed his mother lightly on her forehead before taking his own place.

Charlotte loved this room with its heavy dark furniture gleaming with years of good care, and the high shadowy ceiling soaring into coolness. White walls and wide arched windows shaded by overhanging balconies added to the overall coolness, and the harsh sunlight outside was filtered and diffused before it entered the room by heavy vines of bougainvillea and yellow roses.

The sound of a fountain in the tree-shaded garden made a soft and gentle background to conversation, and the mingled scents of roses, carnations and of orange and lemon blossom wafted in on the warm air. The cool richness of the room and the heavily scented air always gave Charlotte a wonderful sense of well-being, and she had never in her life enjoyed meals as she did here, in these exotic but friendly surroundings.

Martha Berganza looked across the long table set with gleaming silver and exquisite glass, and smiled. She was a good-looking woman, smooth-faced and fair, though her hair was turning grey as she neared fifty, and she was much more plump than Charlotte's mother at the same age, with rather beautiful grey eyes and a warm smile.

She looked at her son with a kind of doting affection that still allowed for shortcomings. Luis was the centre of her existence since the death of her husband, and she had great plans for him. 'You look very smart and businesslike, darling,' she told him, and Luis looked across at Charlotte and pulled a face.

'So Charlotte has already told me, Mamá. You might almost have rehearsed the same lines with the idea of encouraging me!'

'Now, Luis!' She knew her son's reluctance well enough, and it troubled her that he did not apply himself to his profession with the same enthusiasm his father had. 'You'll like working with Don Agustin, you know you will, you've always liked him.'

Luis helped himself to coffee and did not look at her. 'I also like Señora Blanco who keeps the village *tienda*, Mamá, but I haven't the slightest wish to work for her!'

29

'That isn't the same thing at all, Luis, and you know it.'

Martha always treated her son's dislikes with a gentle tolerance that nevertheless hid a very strong determination, and he must have known, Charlotte thought as she looked at him briefly through her lashes, that he had little chance of getting out of the appointment with Don Agustin.

Luis looked at his mother gloomily, then flicked a glance across the table at Charlotte before he took the first sip of his coffee. 'You do not yet realise, Mamá, that it's quite possible I shall find Charlotte lost to me for good if I am to be away from home all day and every day.' His mother looked at him curiously, suspecting some excuse for dodging the coming interview, but Charlotte thought she knew what he had in mind and she carefully avoided looking at him. 'Now that she has met Don Gerardo do you think he will let the matter rest at a few minutes' conversation? I shall be a loser before I have even begun!'

'Don Gerardo?' Martha turned to Charlotte inquiringly, in time to see the reproachful look she sent Luis for his indiscretion. 'Have you met Don Gerardo, my dear? When was this?'

'Yesterday afternoon,' Charlotte replied promptly, before Luis could say anything more about it. 'I almost ran him down with my bicycle.'

'Good heavens!' Martha seemed to have lost interest in her breakfast and was much more curious about her meeting with Don Gerardo. 'What on earth happened, Charlotte? Was he hurt?'

'Not in the least,' Charlotte replied. 'In fact he seemed to find it rather amusing when I asked the same question.' She recalled that brief glimpse of amusement in the black eyes of the man who had dumped her so unceremoniously in the gutter. 'I was the one who came off worst, in fact—though it was my own fault for taking that corner into the village so fast and without looking where I was going.'

Luis took up the story, adding his own touch of drama as he was wont to do with most things. 'He seemed to think he was still performing in the bullring,' he explained to his mother, 'and he picked up Charlotte while she was still on her bike and swung her round as if he was using the *muleta*; then dumped her in the gutter, would you credit?'

'Oh, Charlotte my dear!' Martha's kindly face wore an anxious expression. She was well aware of her son's penchant for exaggeration, but she was bound to believe that there was some truth in what he said. 'Are you sure you weren't hurt? For a man like Don Gerardo it seems a most—ungentlemanly thing to have done. I know he's very autocratic and very much the *amo* in San Cristóbal, but that certainly doesn't give him the right to—to manhandle you in that way.'

'Oh, I'd hardly call it manhandling, Aunt Martha.' Charlotte did her best to counteract the impression Luis had given her, and she glanced at him once more across the table. 'You know how Luis exaggerates! I simply had a close call, that's all, and Don Gerardo reacted quite instinctively when he grabbed my bicycle the way he did. I wasn't hurt and neither was he, fortunately.'

Luis refused to let the drama be minimised, however, and his dark glance dared Charlotte to argue with what he said next. 'Then he stood talking with her for several minutes, instead of going on his way once he had made sure she was unhurt. Does that make sense to you, Mamá?'

Martha said nothing for a second, then she smiled and shook her head. 'To me it does, darling,' she told her son, 'and to you too, I think, but I understand your concern. For a man like Don Gerardo to stand talking to a young lady he has not been formally introduced to, and in a public place too, is rather unusual.'

Luis's dark eyes gleamed with indignant resentment, and Charlotte wished he did not take it all so seriously. 'It is clear that he wished to make the acquaintance of a beautiful girl and he made the most of an opportunity that was heaven-sent for his purpose!'

Charlotte felt colour in her cheeks when she realised how much he read into the meeting, and it made it worse because the same kind of suspicion had entered her own head, only to be hastily dismissed. 'I don't know why you're making so much of it, Luis,' she told him. 'Anyone would think the man had tried to carry me off to his castle, to hear you talk—all we did was have a few moments' conversation.'

'It is rather odd for all that, my dear.' Martha's normally smooth brow was creased with a frown, and Charlotte glanced from her to Luis, her own mind working along the same lines again.

Shaking her head impatiently, she dismissed the idea of Gerardo having designs on her as highly unlikely. What was more, this was the twentieth century, not the Middle Ages, and no one, not even a wealthy and powerful man like Don Gerardo Cortez, could do anything very dramatic with his own village people looking on. She was letting Luis's sense of the dramatic influence her.

'Oh, Aunt Martha, he talked to me, that's all!' She

laughed and shook her head. 'I've been spoken to by strange men before.'

Luis looked vaguely shocked, and eyed her for a moment rather doubtfully. 'Have you?' he asked.

'Well, of course she has, darling,' Martha told him. 'I'm sure you've done your share of chatting up pretty girls, so please don't look so virtuous. Girls as pretty as Charlotte always get approached by men, and whatever else he might be, there's no doubt at all that Don Gerardo is very definitely a man!'

'With a reputation for lechery!' Luis retorted, obviously resenting his own activities being mentioned. 'I'm surprised you are taking this so lightly, Mamá!'

Martha shook her head over his anger. His taste for passion and dramatising were something he inherited from his father, something very Spanish, and she could not think of blaming him for it, but Charlotte thought she sometimes found it hard to deal with. 'Luis dear, I just don't think it's as serious as you seem determined to make it, that's all. I'm sure Don Gerardo behaved perfectly properly towards Charlotte, didn't he, my dear?'

'Perfectly,' Charlotte assured her, anxious to have the matter closed. 'There was really no chance for him to be other than well behaved with two respectable elderly ladies within calling distance all the time.'

'That part does rather puzzle me,' Martha confessed, and Luis was still frowning. 'Why he stopped to talk to you as he did.'

'I don't quite see,' Charlotte ventured, 'why it matters quite so much. I nearly knocked the man over and in the circumstances he was quite entitled to swear at me if he felt inclined. I'm just grateful that instead he helped me up and gave me what was a quite mild lecture considering all things.'

'Did he not suggest that he would like to see you again?' Luis demanded, not easily convinced and obviously feeling he had the right to make such demands, and Charlotte shook her head.

Don Gerardo had mentioned that he hoped it would be in less dangerous circumstances that they met next time, but she chose not to mention that. 'No, he didn't.'

It must have been something in her voice, Charlotte supposed, for Luis was frowning again and his dark eyes held hers for a moment, almost as if he saw himself as a jealous boy-friend with plenty of grounds for suspicion. 'Would you have agreed if he had?' he asked, and his mother made a murmur of protest.

'Luis!'

Charlotte, however, angled her chin in a way that defied him to even ask the question, and her blue eyes had a deep, glowing look that should have warned him she resented his air of possessiveness. 'Quite probably I would have,' she told him, '*if* he'd asked me— he's a very attractive man!'

'Oh, Charlotte dear, I really don't think——' Martha's kindly face was anxious now, and it was obvious that she could not decide whether her answer was merely bravado or if she meant what she said, so that Charlotte smiled at her reassuringly.

'Oh, don't worry, Aunt Martha, it's very unlikely I shall ever see Don Gerardo again to speak to, and it's even more unlikely that he'd suggest anything like you have in mind, even if I did. I imagine he has much more sophisticated tastes than an English girl on a bicycle!'

It was an unheard-of thing to have to jump for one's

life on the dusty little road through San Cristóbal, but Charlotte did so only just in time, letting out a cry of protest as a big black car swept past her as she rounded the corner at the bottom of the hill where she had so nearly come to grief on her bicycle only a few days ago.

She was on foot because a puncture needed mending on the front tyre and she had little or no skill in that direction. She had been day-dreaming, she supposed, as she came down into the village, but for all that she thought she recognised both the car and its driver in the few seconds they were so dangerously close to her.

She half expected to have the car's horn blasted at her in recrimination, but there was nothing of that sort, and she was recovered enough after a second or two to be indignant at the close call. Don Gerardo had not been backward in reprimanding her for the careless way she rode her bicycle, but to her eyes it seemed his own handling of his vehicle was at fault this time.

A shrieking squeal of tyres on the dusty road was a prelude to another confrontation, and Charlotte felt herself shrink inwardly at the prospect. Don Gerardo got out of the car and came striding towards her, covering the distance in a few long strides while she stood there, one hand holding on to the little white hat that at least gave some concealing shadow to her face.

For a second or two the black eyes regarded her steadily from the shadow of thick lashes, a feature she had failed to notice on their first encounter. It was a harsh face, she realised with a small uncontrollable shiver, and the mouth had a hint of cruelty. His clothes were impeccable; expensively tailored and fitting closely enough to emphasise lean hips and long straight legs, and the dazzling whiteness of his shirt made his complexion appear even more darkly golden in contrast.

He was a disturbing and alarmingly arresting figure to meet unexpectedly, and she was not quite sure how to react. Her first reaction had been indignation because he had so nearly run her down, but somehow he was not the kind of man who was easy to blame, especially not by way of a verbal dressing down such as she had had in mind initially.

'So, Señorita Grey, we meet again!' His head bobbed in a brief and very formal bow, but somehow the formality of it was belied by the gleaming darkness of those almost black eyes as they watched her. 'You seem bent upon self-destruction!'

'You can hardly blame me this time!' Charlotte declared, her indignation rekindled. 'You almost ran me down, *señor*!'

One black brow seemed to express surprise at her attitude, and it occurred to her that he was probably not accustomed to being spoken to quite so forcefully. 'I seem to recall that you did the same thing to me only a few days ago, *señorita*,' he reminded her, and it struck her, quite irrelevantly, that his voice was yet another feature of his fascination. It was soft and deep, but at the same time it suggested steel not too far below the velvet, and he probably would not take kindly to an argument that was likely to go against him.

She supposed it was because she was still rather shaken by the near disaster that she spoke without stopping to think first, looking up at him a little dazedly. 'That surely isn't why you——'

'*Zape!* Do you take me for a madman, *señorita*?'

It was the oath that startled her into realising that she had virtually accused him of deliberately trying to run her down, and she hastened to correct the impression, shaking her head urgently. 'Oh no, of course not! I'm sorry if I gave the wrong impression—I didn't mean to suggest you did it on purpose.'

'I would hope not!'

The black eyes gave the discomforting impression of being able to see right through her, and she found it a curiously disturbing sensation so that she hastily lowered her own gaze before them. It was difficult to see what else she could do now but accept that at least some of the blame was hers, although she did not really see it that way, and it rather went against the grain to eat humble pie as she had the last time their paths crossed.

'I suppose it was partly my fault,' she allowed, and noted the arched brow that questioned her obvious reluctance.

'I must agree, *señorita*, for I cannot imagine how you failed to hear my approach. A car engine is surely more readily audible than a bicycle. However, I am relieved to see that once more you are unhurt—you must surely have a guardian angel!'

'Possibly, Don Gerardo, though he obviously has opposition!'

The retort was impulsive and Charlotte regretted it almost before the words were out of her mouth. Don Gerardo certainly resented it, for his black brows drew together in a straight angry line above his glittering eyes. 'You appear to be under the impression that I was at fault in each instance,' he suggested, and the velvet voice now betrayed more of the cold steel.

Once more, as she had during their first encounter, Charlotte felt suddenly and inexplicably small and insignificant as she bore that glittering scrutiny, and she could do nothing about the instinct that urged her to make amends, however little hope there was of his being magnanimous. She did not understand her own reaction, and in some curious way she resented it, but there seemed little else to do but follow her inclinations.

'I—I suppose it *was* my fault again,' she allowed. 'I wasn't expecting anything on this road and I didn't look or listen, I just walked into the road.' Using her eyes the way she did was purely instinctive and not in the least deliberate in this instance. 'I'm sorry, Don Gerardo.'

He said nothing, but neither did he make any attempt to leave, a fact that she noted with a slightly breathless sense of anticipation. Instead he eyed her for a moment in a frank and disconcerting appraisal, then he shook his head and she thought the wide and slightly cruel-looking mouth twitched briefly in to a ghost of a smile.

'Then shall we consider the matter closed?' he suggested, and Charlotte nodded silently, thankful to have it ended without further exchanges. 'May I perhaps convey you to your home, Señorita Grey. In that way,' he added smoothly when he saw her blink of surprise, 'I may be sure that we shall not be in collision on your return journey!'

Charlotte was at a loss to understand exactly why she actually wanted to drive back with him, and her shaking head was as much a denial of her own wayward instincts as a refusal of his offer to drive her. 'I—I have to get stamps for Señora Berganza,' she explained in a curiously unsteady voice. 'I don't know how long I shall be. If——'

'I am in no hurry, *señorita*. If you would like me to

drive you to your home I will do so when you have completed your errand for the *señora*.'

Charlotte's head was spinning when she tried to think of the impression it would make on Martha Berganza to have her secretary arrive home in Don Gerardo's car. Luis's reaction was in no doubt at all if he learned of it—he would dislike the idea intensely.

'It's very kind of you, Don Gerardo, thank you.' She did not see what else she could do but accept, apart from the fact that she did not want to refuse. In her heart she was delighted with the opportunity and it startled her to realise how fast and urgently her heart was hammering in her breast when he nodded his apparent satisfaction.

'*Muy bien*—I will wait for you here.'

In full view of anyone who cared to put two and two together, Charlotte thought dazedly as she crossed the road to the little post office. Already a brown-faced old woman with sharp black eyes had noted their meeting and would probably pass on the news to her cronies. What Don Gerardo did was bound to be of interest to the people of San Cristóbal, and especially if it concerned the English *señorita* who sometimes rode in the car of Señora Berganza's son.

When she came out again it would not have surprised her too much to find him gone, and the whole episode a figment of her imagination brought on by too much sun, but he was still there. A tall and arrogantly casual figure in a light suit leaned against the bonnet of the long black car, and she felt her senses react with that same alarming urgency again.

He discarded a long black cheroot he was smoking, when she reappeared, and he saw her into the passenger seat with a hand under her arm, solicitous and polite, yet curiously detached. She found him even more disturbing when he slid on to the seat beside her and brought the engine to life, and the move she made to edge as far away from him as possible was a kind of defensive reaction against her too responsive senses.

He glanced at her over his shoulder as they drove away from the village, and she thought he smiled, but she did not look at him for long enough to be sure. 'You do not trust me.' He made the observation as if he had no doubt at all that it was true. 'Why is that, *señorita*?'

It was a difficult question to answer, and Charlotte felt rather as if she had been cornered. She supposed she did not entirely trust him, though he had given her no reason not to as yet; most likely those rather biassed opinion's of Luis's had made her wary of him. Luis's uncomplimentary opinion of him, she had to admit, would not altogether surprise her if it proved to be true, but she should not allow her judgment to be formed on what was in all probability nothing more than hearsay.

Don Gerardo Cortez was a very attractive man; mature and sophisticated and most likely irresistible to a lot of women, so who could blame him if he made the most of his natural attributes? For her own part, she had no intention of letting herself be affected by that worldly charm, and she thought she was at least half way to remaining cool-headed simply by being aware of his attractions and controlling her own responses.

'I don't know why you should think I don't trust you, Don Gerardo,' she told him, her voice carefully controlled, and once more he directed a brief glance over his shoulder.

'I think perhaps you have—heard of me.' A slight but very expressive shrug of his broad shoulders conveyed his meaning far more explicitly than words, and she found herself wishing she had been better prepared for this kind of conversation.

'I don't listen to gossip, Don Gerardo!'

It was the only answer she could find on the spur of the moment and she started visibly when he gave a short and very sceptical laugh. 'Then you are a most unusual woman, *señorita*!'

The run from the village took little enough time on her bicycle, it seemed no time at all in the powerful black sports car, and Charlotte stared at the familiar gateway of Casa Berganza as if she did not believe they had arrived already. She expected him to get out and open the car door for her, he would afford that formal politeness to anyone, even though he had just accused her of listening to gossip about him. What she did not expect was that he would cut the engine, then turn in his seat and face her, his strong dark features carefully impassive.

Charlotte felt her heart begin a hard, frantic beat that arose from both panic and excitement, and she wondered if she had been wise to accept a lift from him after all. The black eyes were unfathomable and yet there was a glow in their depths that suggested an emotion of some kind barely suppressed.

He said nothing for a moment, and she wondered rather wildly if it would be possible for her to open the door and get out without his taking any action to prevent her. 'Thank you, Don Gerardo.' Her voice had a shivering sound of uncertainty that he could not fail to notice.

'You work as a secretary, I believe, Señorita Grey?'

41

Once more he surprised her into momentary silence, and she stared at him for a second before she answered. 'Yes—yes, I do.'

What possible bearing it could have on anything, she could not imagine, unless he was simply curious to know exactly what she was in the Berganza household. He was perhaps wondering if Luis had some kind of claim to her.

'You like working in Spain?' This time she merely nodded, and he swept that inscrutable gaze over her face. 'I have new business interests in England,' the velvet soft voice went on, 'I need an English secretary who has some small knowledge of Spanish, Señorita Grey—you have that?'

Charlotte stared at him wide-eyed. Her heart was thudding in her breast and there was a bright flush of colour in her cheeks when she realised at last the reason for his interest in her. 'You mean——' She swallowed hard, her voice almost failing. 'You're asking if I'll— if I'll leave Señora Berganza and work—for you?'

She had thought his mouth cruel when she estimated his character earlier, and she had further cause to think so now when she saw the way it flicked tightly into the mockery of a smile. The black eyes glowed with what could only be amusement, and he shook his head slowly. Her flush of colour, her evasive eyes showed him plainly enough what interpretation she had put on his interest in her, and she felt a curling coldness inside suddenly as he watched her.

Turned in his seat to face her, he was too close for comfort, and she had an almost panicky desire to be as far away from him as possible. Reaching for the door handle, she tried in vain to open it until a large hand reached across her, bringing him into close contact with her as he leaned forward, strong hard fingers enclosing her own trembling ones as well as the door handle and pressing down until it opened.

'I will not question what reasons you imagined I had for approaching you, *señorita*.' The quietness of his voice somehow added to her embarrassment and she bit on her lower lip hard and kept her head turned from him. 'I *will* ask that you consider working for me —will you?'

It startled her to realise that the appeal was well-nigh irresistible, and she got out hastily on to the hot dusty road, standing on legs that were horribly unsteady, like her voice as she sought hard to control it. 'I'm quite happy here with Señora Berganza, thank you, Don Gerardo.'

'*Muy bien.*' The broad shoulders shrugged lightly as he slammed the car door and a second later Charlotte was already at the gate, even though he still sat there. 'If you should have a change of mind, Señorita Grey,' he called out to her, 'you will know where I am to be found.'

Turning in the gateway, Charlotte looked across at him for a moment. She felt strangely shattered by the events of the last few minutes and the realisation troubled her, for it should not matter so much that a stranger had offered her work rather than the more intimate proposition she had expected. She had already told him that she preferred to stay on with Martha Berganza, and yet she found herself curiously reluctant to reject his offer out of hand.

'Yes, I know,' she said.

Black eyes gleamed in the strong, dusky golden features, and he raised a hand in salute as the car moved off along the road. '*Hasta la vista!*' The words came back to her on the hot, dusty air, heavy with the scent of oranges, and she did not bother to speculate whether or not they would meet again as he suggested—it was almost inevitable.

CHAPTER THREE

LUIS's interview with his father's old friend had been as successful as it was expected to be, and he had started work in the office of Don Agustin almost at once. There had been little doubt of the outcome, of course, for Luis had done well in his exams, and the place for him in Don Agustin's firm had been assured in the event of his qualifying. Charlotte was delighted because she knew how deeply concerned Martha was that he should do well for his father's sake.

Charlotte had said nothing so far about Don Gerardo's startlingly unexpected offer of employment, and she was not sure she ever would. For one thing she found it embarrassing, after Luis's remarks, to have to realise and admit that Don Gerardo's interest in her had never been other than purely and simply on a business level. Martha would probably worry too, in case she thought of accepting, and Luis would almost certainly refuse to believe that a job as secretary was all that was being offered.

Lately Luis's attitude towards her had become increasingly more serious, until Charlotte sometimes wondered if she would one day be faced with the need to give up her job with Martha because she did not feel romantically enough about her son. During the day, while Luis was at work, there was no problem, but at evenings and week-ends it was a different story.

Martha was bound to have noticed her son's increasing attentiveness, and while they sat drinking coffee together one morning she teased Charlotte about it. 'You've completely captivated Luis, of course,' she told her, and her eyes were warm and friendly, making it clear that she was not averse to the idea in the least. 'You realise, don't you, that any day now he'll be proposing to you?'

'Oh, I do hope not!' She spoke without thinking, and saw the way Martha stared at her in stunned surprise. It was not the response she expected, of course, and she would not understand her reaction at all. 'I mean,' Charlotte went on hastily, 'that I hate the thought of hurting Luis's feelings, and I'm really not ready to be proposed to by anyone yet, however dishy he is.'

'You think Luis is dishy?' Martha asked, knowing the answer full well, and Charlotte nodded.

'Oh, but of course he is—he's good-looking, and he's *nice* too, it's a fairly rare combination.'

'But you don't want to marry him?'

It wasn't easy to explain her feelings to his mother, who saw him as the ideal man and one that any girl would give her right arm to marry. But it simply would not be right to let things develop between her and Luis when she knew in her heart that she did not love him enough to marry him—not yet, anyway.

'I don't want to marry anyone yet, Aunt Martha, not even Luis, and he's easily the best looking and the nicest person I know.'

Martha Berganza's grey eyes were clouded with disappointment as she set down her coffee cup carefully beside her, and Charlotte wished the subject had never been raised. She hated disappointing anyone, and she was very fond of this plump and rather pretty woman.

'I'm disappointed, Charlotte, I won't pretend I'm not, but you know your own mind best and you're honest enough not to accept simply because Luis is, although I say it, a good catch.' She smiled a little warily. 'Perhaps in a little while——'

'Perhaps.' Charlotte refused to make any rash promises, much as she was tempted so as not to hurt someone who so obviously wanted her for her daughter-in-law—it was a rare compliment and she recognised it. She finished her own coffee and put down her cup. 'I'm sorry, Aunt Martha.'

The older woman reached across and squeezed her fingers, at the same time shaking her head. 'Oh no, my dear, you have nothing to apologise for. None of us can dictate to our hearts, and certainly no one else has the right to try to—even doting mothers!'

Charlotte smiled. 'I'd have to be sure, otherwise it wouldn't be fair, would it?'

'Of course you must be sure! I met and married Luis's father and I never had a second's doubt that he was the man for me, but then there was never anyone but Federigo—I suppose I was lucky.'

'It must have been a wonderful marriage.'

Whenever Martha spoke of her husband or her marriage there was a kind of glow about her, as if even now he was no longer there they still shared a special kind of love. It was the kind of love that Charlotte hoped she would find one day, when she was ready to fall in love and marry.

'It *was* a wonderful marriage,' Martha agreed, soft-voiced, 'and I hope Luis will be as lucky when he marries.'

46

'I'm sure he will be—he deserves to be.' For some reason beyond her understanding it was not Luis's good looks but the dark strong face of Don Gerardo Cortez that came into her mind at that moment, and she sought hastily for a change of subject. 'I was wondering how the young people around here manage to have any social life,' she said. 'They don't have much opportunity to mix, not like we do at home, do they?'

Martha's smile beamed at her mischievously, and she rolled her eyes with unmistakable meaning as she shook her head. 'Oh, they manage well enough,' she assured her. 'There are quite a few weddings in a year and any number of christenings! Love will always find a way, my dear.'

'Yes—yes, I suppose it will.'

Charlotte answered absently, mostly because yet again the dark brooding features of Don Gerardo Cortez had come unbidden into her mind, and her vagueness must have struck Martha, for she was leaning forward in her chair, and touching her hand lightly. 'Charlotte, my dear, is there something worrying you? Is there anything you want to talk to me about?' Noting Charlotte's curious frown, she shook her head hastily. 'I'm sorry, my dear, I promise you I haven't been prying, I wouldn't dream of interfering in anything you do—you must realise that.'

'Yes, of course, I realise it, Aunt Martha.' Some inkling of what was on Martha Berganza's mind made her wary, and she looked at her curiously.

'Charlotte——' Her eyes were anxious, but she still hesitated to say what was on her mind. 'Padre Larraga saw you with Don Gerardo one day last week—he said you drove off in his car with him.'

'And he told you?' She resented it and the resent-

47

ment showed in her eyes, although she in no way blamed Martha for the village priest's interest in her affairs.

'He thought I should know because he was doubtful if you were aware of Don Gerardo's—reputation, my dear,' Martha explained gently, and sought to soothe over her resentment. 'He meant well and he was genuinely anxious that you should realise what kind of man you were apparently making friends with.'

She did not mean making friends, any more than the the priest had, Charlotte thought, and recalled her own misconception in the matter of Don Gerardo's intentions towards her. The rather bitter sound of her laughter was unconscious and Martha noted it with a frown.

'Oh, not friendly, Aunt Martha, nor—whatever it is Don Gerardo has a reputation for! His interest in me is purely a business one!'

Martha was both puzzled and uneasy, her expression made that perfectly clear. 'Business? My dear, what *do* you mean?'

'I mean that Don Gerardo asked me to leave you and to go and work for him,' Charlotte told her. 'He offered me a job, Aunt Martha.'

'But——' Martha looked as if she found it hard to believe, 'I don't understand, Charlotte. Do you mean to say that Don Gerardo approached you as he did simply to suggest that you go and work for him?'

'That's exactly what I mean!' She could barely restrain a smile when she thought of the priest, so concerned about Don Gerardo's intentions, when his suspicions could not have been further from the truth. 'He drove me home after nearly running me down in the village,' she explained. 'I know that sounds rather too much of a coincidence after what happened the first time, but it's true. He stopped to make sure I was all right, then offered me a lift; he even insisted on waiting while I bought your stamps from the post office. It wasn't until we got here, right at the gates, that he sprang the offer of a job on me.'

'You said no, of course?' Anxiety tinged her voice and Charlotte hastened to reassure her.

'I said no,' she agreed. 'But it was so unexpected, Aunt Martha, that I didn't know what to say to him at first, I was too—too stunned.' She looked at the older woman for a moment, unable to diguise her interest in the man she seemed literally to bump into at every turn. 'I didn't know he was a business man, I thought he was simply an autocratic landowner with an appetite for female company.' It wasn't quite the truth, but it gave a general impression and it served in part to cover her interest.

'He's all three, my dear.' There was a tight look about Martha's mouth that spoke of disapproval. 'I suppose one should feel sympathy for him, for he can't have had a very happy time during most of his life, but somehow Gerardo Cortez isn't a man who attracts sympathy, he's too much the *amo*—too much the lord and master, in that massive castle of his.'

'*Has* he had an unhappy life?' Charlotte was not at the moment making any attempt to disguise her interest, and she was aware of Martha's frown.

'I know nothing about the man except what Federigo told me a long time ago,' Martha said, 'and I shouldn't repeat old gossip, Charlotte.'

Remembering his retort when she had denied listening to gossip, Charlotte smiled wryly. 'You'd be a most unusual woman if you didn't,' she quoted, and noticed a blink of surprise when she laughed.

'I suppose it's a feminine trait,' Martha allowed.

'So is curiosity, Aunt Martha, and I frankly admit that I'm curious about Gerardo Cortez.'

Briefly and anxiously Martha's grey eyes scanned her face, then she shook her head. 'Charlotte, you're not——'

'No, I'm not—really!' She smiled at Martha confidently. 'He's a very attractive man, but I shan't go walking blindfold into that particular spider's web, you may be sure of it, Aunt Martha. I'm just curious, that's all.'

'He *is* a fascinating man,' Martha agreed cautiously, 'but he's a dangerous one too, and you're very young, Charlotte. I promised your mother——'

'I'm twenty-three, Aunt Martha, and very sane and sensible.' She smiled encouragingly. 'I promise I won't work for him, or elope with him or anything else silly, but I *am* curious, so will you please tell me why you say he's had an unhappy life.'

It was clear that Martha would rather not have passed on the stories her husband had told her, but she did so because she sensed that a refusal would only make Charlotte more curious. 'It mostly concerned his father,' she told her. 'He fell in love with the girl that one of his cousins was betrothed to, and stayed single for eighteen years until she was widowed.'

'He waited all that time for her?' To Charlotte the idea was infinitely touching and she looked eagerly for the outcome. 'But that was a happy ending, surely?'

'By the time a decent interval had elapsed and they were married, Don Rafael was over fifty and the lady over forty,' Martha explained. 'Of course they wanted one child if no more, it was natural in the circumstances, but it was dangerous too, and Señora Cortez died when their son was born.'

'Oh, what a tragedy!'

'In a way it was a double tragedy,' Martha told her, 'for Don Rafael the loss was unbearable and he became unbalanced. He never recovered and he lingered on until two years ago. Don Gerardo inherited it all, of course, though unfortunately he hasn't inherited his father's sense of propriety. He's never married, but he's never short of female company and doesn't seem to mind who knows it, though at least he has the decency not to parade his conquests in San Cristóbal.'

'Did his father know about—the way he is?'

Martha pursed her lips, as if she gave the praise grudgingly. 'No, to give him his due he was very good and patient with his father, so I believe, and Don Rafael knew nothing about his—affairs.'

In which case it seemed rather harsh to condemn him, Charlotte felt, although she realised that the Spanish view of promiscuity was rather more severe than was fashionable in some countries, and in twenty-six years Martha Berganza's outlook had possibly become more Spanish than she realised.

Not that Gerardo Cortez was likely to concern himself with anyone's opinion of him. He was strong and arrogant, and self-sufficient enough to treat with contempt any suggestion of sympathy, she felt sure. No doubt he would take himself a wife one day, for that huge gloomy fortress of a castle would need another Cortez to carry on its traditions, and she could imagine him as a man with a sense of family tradition no matter what his personal tastes were. She did not envy the woman who accepted him, Charlotte thought, and would be expected to cope with that great sombre

51

building and its master—it would take a brave woman and a dedicated one.

'I imagine he'll marry one day,' she suggested, and hurried on when Martha looked at her curiously. 'To have someone to leave in his place—the next generation of Cortez.'

'Oh, yes, I suppose he will.' She shook her head and made a wry face as she looked across at Charlotte. 'He's a fascinating man, a very attractive one, but it will take a very tolerant woman to put up with him. It will need to be a Spanish woman, they have the right temperament to cope.'

'Yes, yes, I suppose it will.' She was not aware of anything in her voice that made Martha look at her sharply. 'I imagine he would prefer one of his own race anyway.'

It was a couple of days later that Charlotte organised a solitary day out. Until now she had always had Luis for company whenever she went anywhere except into the village, and the idea of wandering around Arcos de la Frontera for a couple of hours or so on her own appealed to her.

Martha was visiting friends and Luis would of course be required at his office, so she could enjoy her free time in whatever way she liked. It had been agreed that Luis would drive her in with him, and that he would meet her for lunch about half-past two, so that she would have plenty of time to do whatever she wanted.

He drove with a certain panache, which she supposed was part of the Latin character, and the drive in to Arcos was pleasant, despite the state of the road for much of the journey. Arcos de la Frontera was built on the crest of a hill overlooking the Guadalete valley and was, so Luis claimed, the prettiest town in Spain, a claim that Charlotte saw no reason to argue with, for it was a delightful place and very Spanish.

Its wide streets were shaded and bordered by ancient buildings, and three of the ancient gateways still existed, and it was delightfully medieval in character. Except for the motor traffic in the streets she felt she might have been transported back several hundred years, and she was quite happy to have an hour or two on her own to explore it. Luis, on the other hand, let it be known that he would have been happier about the whole thing if he had been keeping her company.

'But I'm quite capable of finding my way around alone, Luis!' She smiled at his disgruntled expression and shook her head. 'There are no end of tourists about, and most of the shop people speak at least some English. I shan't get lost.'

'Just the same I'd be happier if I was coming with you,' he insisted. 'You're much too pretty to be walking around on your own, Charlotte.'

'But I walk around on my own at home in England!'

Luis frowned. 'That's not the same thing at all.'

'Don't you trust me among all your dark-eyed compatriots?' Her smile teased him, but she realised how seriously he was taking it when she saw the way his eyes gleamed and the frown that drew black brows together.

'It is not that I don't trust you, Charlotte but in Spain sometimes English girls are considered to be less—reserved than our own girls,' he told her with a hint of rebuke. 'If someone should think——'

'No one will!' Charlotte assured him hastily. 'Now please stop worrying about me, Luis, and go, before Don Agustin thinks you've given yourself the day off.

Please,' she added firmly when he looked like arguing the matter further, and Luis shrugged.

'I'll go, but I don't like seeing you go off alone, Charlotte.' He stood looking at her for a moment longer, then shrugged his shoulders once again, and turned back to his car. '*Muy bien,*' he said, 'I see that it is no use my trying to dissuade you. But please, Charlotte, don't be late for our lunch appointment or I shall be thinking that my fears have been realised.'

'Of course I won't be late!' She smiled at him as he slid in behind the wheel once more, then pulled the little white hat more firmly on over her fair hair. ''Bye, Luis!'

He started up the engine and she waved a hand when he drove past her a second later, a short, sharp blast on the horn reminding her of her promise. If ever she allowed things to get more serious between herself and Luis, she thought ruefully, he would prove a jealous lover, and she was not sure she liked the idea of that very much. Not, she reminded herself, that she had any intention of letting things get any more serious for a long time yet.

As it happened she did very little actual shopping, but she enjoyed herself enormously just looking into shop windows, and wandering around looking at the beautiful old buildings. It was too much to resist a visit to the old castle that had once housed the conquering Moorish kings, and she sat on the parapet for some time, letting her mind wander over the history of the place. It was almost without realising it that she suddenly found herself thinking about Don Gerardo Cortez.

He was descended from the same conquering Moors, and he still lived in a huge fortress-like castle perched on a pinnacle of rock above the valley, just as this one was. In these circumstances it was all too easy to visualise him in the role of lord of all he surveyed—which in his case included the village of San Cristóbal.

From the parapet she could look down at the river Guadalete as it swept round below her like the curve of a scimitar, or gaze at the distance where the heat-shrouded mountains stood like giant sand castles, arid and barren above the fertile plains that thrived on the mountain water. Birds hovered in the still, hot air above the valley, birds of prey, she thought, and was once more reminded of Gerardo Cortez. It was a strangely wild but intriguing landscape and one into which a man like him fitted perfectly.

She brought herself hastily back to earth with an audible sigh although she could find no tangible reason for sighing so deeply, and as she turned from the scene to walk back into the town, she became aware of someone watching her. It was a curious, edgy sensation there was no mistaking, and it drew her gaze unerringly to the watcher. It was a second or two before she fully realised the unmistakable meaning in the smile he sent her.

He was quite young and passably good-looking, but the boldness in the dark eyes was like a warning that brought all Luis's anxious words flooding back to her. Having drawn her attention, the young man evidently took her brief curious look as an invitation to make more definite advances, and he was already walking along to join her before Charlotte was fully aware of the situation.

Turning hastily, she started back along the parapet, seeking the temporary company of a party of French tourists that she had passed earlier, but the soft sound of her pursuer's footsteps followed her as she hurried off, and she veered instead in the other direction.

It was annoyance, not fear, that made her try and evade him, for there were plenty of people about and she did not believe he had any other intent in mind except the one which showed so plainly in his eyes. Also she preferred not to have to reject his advances verbally if she could avoid it, for she had the Anglo-Saxon dislike of public scenes. Much better retreat than stay and tell him that he had the wrong idea about her.

'Señorita!' He was nearer and more insistent than she had realised, and the party of French tourists was some distance off by now.

Glancing hastily over her shoulder, she hurried on, deciding to leave him in no doubt of her opinion. 'Please go away!' She sought the equivalent Spanish words, and hoped he was going to be more easily persuable than his appearance suggested. '*Marchase, por favor!*'

Dark eyes gleamed and he showed startlingly white teeth in the swarthy darkness of his face as he fell into step beside her. 'Ah, the *señorita* is English—I have good English, *señorita*.' He swept his gaze over her slightly flushed face and laughed softly, as if to himself. 'I am a very good guide, if you come with me I can be much more fun than these old fellows.' He waved a scornful hand in the direction of the two elderly men who were conducting the French party and a German couple, and his lip curled. 'You come with me, *señorita*, huh?'

'No, thank you!' Charlotte hurried on without pausing, but he kept pace with her easily and was apparently unwilling to believe that his company was unwelcome.

'The town of Arcos de la Frontera is my home, *señorita*, I will be your personal guide and show you much that is interesting.'

Once more, as she glanced hastily at him from the corner of her eyes, he left her in no doubt of his real purpose, and she kept right on, making for the shops and the more busy streets of the town. It made her hot walking so quickly, but she felt sure that once she gained the more busy streets where the shops were he would give up, and she was beginning to tire of his persistence.

He showed no sign of giving up, however, and even when she was making her way along the streets of shops he was still beside her so that in desperation she turned into a shop doorway without stopping to see what the place sold. She made a purchase, taking her time over choosing something she had no real use for, but came out again only to find him leaning nonchalantly against the shop window.

He beamed her another smile as she emerged and her face in the shadow of her hat brim flushed with annoyance. He should have recognised the danger signals in her blue eyes, but instead he fell into step with her once more, confident as ever, and smiling when she glanced at him from the corner of her eyes.

'Will you *please* go away!' She faced him on the shaded pavement, still unwilling to make a scene, but rapidly losing patience. 'I don't need a guide and I don't need an escort—please leave me alone!'

'*Señorita!*' He probably meant to do no more than use a hand to express his regret or to emphasise his innocent intent, but to Charlotte his raised hand seemed to represent a threat and she instinctively stepped back and almost off the edge of the kerb. '*Señorita, cuidado!*'

His warning cry attracted the attention of people passing, which was exactly what Charlotte had wanted to avoid, and she was close to losing her temper as she felt herself the focus of several curious eyes. She glanced about her swiftly, then pushed the little white hat more firmly on to her head and looked at him with angry blue eyes.

'If you don't go away and stop bothering me,' she warned, 'I shall call for someone to help me—*la policia*,' she added, to make quite sure he understood.

'But, *señorita*——'

Whatever he had been going to say in his own defence was cut short with startling suddenness and he half turned to go, but before he could take a step, a hand closed over his arm and held him firmly, hard dark fingers digging into him so that there was no chance of his escaping.

A passing *guardia* came to mind, one who had seen her predicament and come to her rescue, and Charlotte turned to thank him, but even before she set eyes on him, his voice had identified him—and she knew it was no *guardia*.

'May I assist you, Señorita Grey? This man is annoying you?'

Too startled for a second to make a sensible answer, Charlotte shook her head, a gesture that brought a swift frown to those dark autocratic features and a gleam of suspicion to the black eyes. His captive was making some hasty explanation in his own tongue, to which Gerardo Cortez listened with obvious disbelief, turning again to look at her when the voluble speech came to an end.

'Is it true that this man is acting as your guide, *señorita?*' he asked, and once more Charlotte shook her head, though with more certainty this time.

'I've been trying to get rid of him ever since I left the castle,' she explained, 'but he just won't take no for an answer.'

The hard fingers on the man's arm tightened cruelly, and there was an edge of steel on the velvet voice that sent an involuntary shiver through her. For a moment she wondered if she should have made light of the incident, instead of being so honest about it, but it seemed it was already too late.

'Then allow me to persuade him,' Don Gerardo said.

He did not wait for her permission, but spoke to the man rapidly but quietly in his own tongue, and from the shadow of her lashes Charlotte saw the contempt that showed in the strong dark face, the disdain that curled his lip. It was a verbal lashing that obviously had the intended effect, for the younger man looked so thoroughly chastened that he almost had her pity.

'*Váyase!*'

The abuse came to an end and the man was curtly dismissed. He needed no second bidding and he sped away through the crowds on the pavement, disappearing almost at once with Charlotte, still slightly dazed by the whole incredible incident, staring after him.

She had been confident when she left Luis that she could cope with anything that happened, and her first surprise had been the persistence of her pursuer, second was the sudden appearance of Don Gerardo and his cool taking over of the situation. Not that she could not have coped, she told herself, but his coming so

59

readily and so fiercely to her rescue gave her a curious sense of satisfaction.

She should thank him, she reminded herself, but somehow it was difficult to know what to say exactly with the black eyes watching her from between thick lashes, curious and vaguely suspicious. 'I—I thought he'd never go,' she said. 'Thank you, Don Gerardo.'

'Please—think nothing of it. I am only sorry that you should have been subjected to such an exhibition of bad manners by one of my countrymen.'

Laughing a little unsteadily, she looked up at him and shook her head. 'It's the kind of thing that can happen anywhere,' she told him, and the black eyes regarded her steadily.

'That is no excuse for it happening here, *señorita*!' He took note of that slightly unsteady laugh and apparently read more into it than she intended. 'Perhaps you are made apprehensive by the incident, Señorita Grey, and would prefer not to continue alone?'

'Oh no, really.' She hastened to reassure him on that point because she could foresee only one outcome if she did not. 'I was annoyed with him, that's all, because he was so persistent.'

'Naturally he was persistent.' A large hand slid beneath her arm and it was clear that he meant to ensure against any further such incidents. He walked beside her with his palm warm and smooth and unbelievably disturbing on her soft skin, his strong fingers curled just lightly enough to remind her of how hard he could grip. 'You are a temptation to a man of that type, Señorita Grey.'

'Unintentionally, I assure you!'

Briefly the black gaze swept over her, from the light open sandals she wore to the white hat covering her

60

corn-gold hair. It was a scrutiny so searching and explicit, despite its brevity, that she caught her breath. 'Intentional or not, you are a temptation to any man, *señorita*, and my countrymen are perhaps more impressionable than your own.'

'Don Gerardo——'

'You are about to return home?' The velvet-soft voice interrupted quietly but firmly, and the strong fingers on her arm curled slightly, digging more firmly into her. 'May I drive you home, *señorita*?'

The offer was as unexpected as it had been the last time he offered to drive her home, and she reacted in much the same way at first, before shaking her head firmly. 'Oh no, thank you, Don Gerardo, I'm seeing Luis—Señor Berganza, for lunch.'

'Ah!' It seemed something had become clear to him, and he was nodding his head. 'I am surprised that he allows you to walk about Arcos unescorted.'

Charlotte flushed, both with embarrassment and annoyance. It was clear that he had quite the wrong idea about her relationship with Luis, and she was anxious to put him right without quite knowing why it mattered so much that a stranger jumped to the wrong conclusion.

'It isn't a case of being allowed, Don Gerardo. I'm a free agent to come and go as I please!'

'So!' A black brow flicked briefly in surprise and the hand on her arm tightened its hold fractionally for a moment. 'You choose to expose yourself to such incidents? You surely do not enjoy being approached in the way that young man approached you just now?'

It was an awkward situation and one which Charlotte would rather have solved somewhere less public than on a busy street; as it was she glanced up into that implaccable dark face and sought hard to keep a hold on her temper. 'I don't walk about with the intention of attracting that kind of thing, Don Gerardo, it's simply that I'm used to——'

'A less impassioned form of admiration, perhaps?' he suggested, soft-voiced, and she glanced up swiftly, suspecting he found the idea in some way amusing.

'Maybe!' she retorted defensively.

He was looking at the heavy gold wristwatch on his arm, and ignored her flash of temper. 'If you are to meet Señor Berganza, may I escort you to the restaurant?' he suggested. 'At what time are you meeting him?'

'Half-past two.' Charlotte consulted her own watch and caught her breath when she saw what time it was. 'Oh, good heavens, I'm late already—Luis will be imagining heaven knows what! He didn't like letting me go without him,' she explained, and caught a brief smile about his mouth when she admitted it.

'But you do not take heed of such advice, eh, Señorita Grey?'

'Really, Don Gerardo, I don't——'

'Where are you to meet Señor Berganza?' He interrupted her yet again in that smooth quiet voice, and the black eyes challenged her to object to it.

'El Castillo,' she replied, and gave an inward sigh of resignation.

'I know it.'

He held her arm firmly and drew her along with him, and it was once again her reluctance to create a scene that stopped her from telling him she could find the restaurant quite easily on her own. There was nothing to dislike about walking through Arcos with a tall, distinguished man like Gerardo Cortez, and she almost began to enjoy the experience when she noticed how much attention he attracted from passing females, however discreet.

She spotted Luis standing outside the restaurant only a second before he saw her with Don Gerardo, and she saw the sudden look of blank surprise in his eyes before they narrowed sharply and a flush coloured his good-looking features. As he came towards them Charlotte tried to draw her arm from the hold of those strong fingers, something that she achieved with unexpected ease, so that by the time Luis met them Gerardo Cortez was no longer touching her.

'Charlotte?' Luis flicked his curious and frankly disapproving glance between them, inclining his head in a brief and coldly polite bow to the man with her. 'You're late, I thought something must have happened to you.'

Trying to make light of the incident wasn't easy with Gerardo Cortez beside her, but she shrugged lightly and smiled at Luis, her eyes teasing. 'Nothing's happened to me, Luis, as you see. I had an unknown admirer for a while, but Don Gerardo got rid of him for me.'

Luis's gaze transferred itself reluctantly to their neighbour's autocratic face and he inclined his head once more, stiffly formal and polite. 'I am indebted to you, Don Gerardo. *Muchas gracias.*'

Don Gerardo merely nodded. His eyes were on Charlotte and it was plain that he was still puzzled about her exact relationship with Luis. Luis's thanks could have left him in little doubt that he felt possessive enough about her to speak as if he had done him a personal service by coming to her aid, but Don

Gerardo, she thought, still questioned her own feelings in the matter.

'Now that you are in safe keeping, *señorita*,' he said, his black eyes holding hers, 'I will leave you—*buenas tardes*.' His head inclined in another brief bow to Luis. '*Buenas tardes, señor*.'

Luis nodded, obviously anxious to have him gone, but to Charlotte there was a strange sense of anti-climax about the parting, and she spoke again as he turned to go. 'Thank you again, Don Gerardo, I really was grateful to you.'

He turned his head, his eyes steady and depthlessly jet black in the dark autocratic features. Then a ghost of a smile flicked at one corner of his mouth for a second before he bobbed another bow. 'It was my pleasure, Señorita Grey—I only hope that when we meet again it will be without incident—*hasta luego*!'

'When you meet again!' Luis declared angrily as he took her arm. 'By what right does he assume you will meet again?'

Charlotte watched the tall arrogant figure of Gerardo Cortez as it disappeared into the crowd, and she shook her head. 'Maybe because it's inevitable,' she suggested.

CHAPTER FOUR

CHARLOTTE had the afternoon free, and without Luis to drive her where she wanted to go she decided to cycle a couple of miles the other side of the village to look at a little church that Martha had told her about. Luis had said he was willing to take her when he was not working, but since she was unlikely to be bothered by unwelcome attentions while visiting a church in the depth of the country, and because she knew he did not really enjoy looking at churches, she chose to go on her own.

It was impossible to miss the little church where it stood cool and silent among the endless olive groves, and she spent some time admiring it, both inside and out. The old *sacristán* had been only too pleased to show her the church's treasures and spoke quite passable English, so that her meagre Spanish was not put to the test.

There were ancient paintings that had decorated the walls for hundreds of years, crude, simple but somehow very beautiful paintings, perhaps executed with more faith than skill, but effective for all that. And the carved stone figures that stood in the niches around the thick walls, illuminated with clusters of candles, like fluttering little symbols of faith.

The old man had enjoyed her company, she thought, and been pleased by her interest, and he had been reluctant to see her go. He shook his head over her thanks, but smiled a gratified, '*Muchas gracias, señorita*,' when he noticed the amount she put into the *ofertorio* when she left.

It would be cooler on the way back, for it lay downhill all the way, and she was creating her own breeze. The soft rose pink cotton dress she wore had sleeves and a discreet neckline, but it was full-skirted enough for easy movement, making it suitable for both cycling and visiting a church.

It also complemented her lightly tanned skin and the bright flaxen fairness of her hair below the inevitable little white hat, and she was brought swiftly back from the spiritual world into the earthly one, not long after leaving the church, by the appreciative calls of a group of young men working in one of the olive groves. Fulsome and rather ribald Spanish flattery followed her progress as she freewheeled down the hill towards San Cristóbal, the voices hard and flat on the dusty air.

The familiar landscape was laid out around and ahead of her. A predominance of pale green crowning the twisted grey trunks of the olives, that was patched here and there by the darker green orange groves, and the little white *casetas* of the village running like a trickle of spilled milk among them. The Casa Berganza was hidden from her by a dip in the landscape and by the trees that surrounded it, but the castle of Don Gerardo Cortez sat perched like a bird of prey on its rock pinnacle, reminding her yet again of the man who lived in it.

It was the first time she had had the opportunity to study it from that angle and with as much time to take note of it as she had today. Luis always drove quite fast and each time she had come with him along that same road, her view of the castle had changed with every second and given her little time to notice details.

There was, she had to admit, a certain gloomy splendour about the rugged walls and the pointed turrets that stabbed upwards into the brassy blue Andalucían sky. Its lower ramparts were softened by a mass of trees, but above them the harsh craggy stone battlements thrust aggressively, glowering over the fertile valley over which its occupiers had ruled for so long, a reminder of the once great power of the Cortez.

It was a stunning sight, and seeing it properly for the first time gave Charlotte a curious thrill of excitement, a sense of history that was thrillingly affecting. It was so right as a home for Gerardo Cortez, and she could not imagine him living in any other surroundings. He was a man out of his time, as that great domineering castle was—a symbol of strength and power that was no longer possible in the modern world, and yet could still inspire a certain awe.

From there, the hill descended sharply into the village, and it took all her wits to avoid the numerous pot holes in the road as she sped downwards. The massive iron gates of Castillo Cortez loomed up on her left, distracting her for no more than a second, while she glanced along the shadowed and overgrown private road, but in the circumstances, a second was long enough.

An unnoticed bump in the road seemed almost to jerk her head from her shoulders when she hit it at full speed, and the front wheel of her bicycle was deflected towards the big iron gates with Charlotte helpless to do anything about it. She felt the bump, experienced an alarming sense of helplessness when the handlebars were wrenched out of her hands, and lost consciousness when her head hit one of the ornately carved gateposts.

After that she could remember only a series of impressions that were none of them clear or of very long duration. Voices speaking in Spanish, and faces looking down at her, hazy and unrecognisable, and at one point a pair of strong arms that lifted her and seemed to carry her quite a distance before they put her down again, gently and carefully.

While she was being carried other impressions kept coming and going. The softness of silk against her cheek, with a curious sensation like the touch of a human body through its softness, and a warm masculine scent that was strange to her and yet oddly familiar; vague, hazy impressions that were disturbing, even to her barely receptive mind.

It was some time before she felt able to open her eyes, but she could appreciate the touch of something ice-cold on her brow and the quiet murmur of voices kept deliberately low. It was the sound of her own name, spoken softly and quite close, that finally brought her out of that not unpleasant state of half-unconsciousness. The sound of it fluttered like a warm breath against her cheek and she drew a deep slow breath and opened her eyes.

The first face she saw was the dark and undeniably anxious one of Gerardo Cortez, and he drew back slightly when she opened her eyes. *'Dios gracias!'* He breathed the pious thanks barely above a whisper, then turned to speak to someone behind him, murmuring something in Spanish that she did not catch.

In answer to his instruction a woman's face appeared over his shoulder, as if she stood immediately behind him; a dark brown and incredibly wrinkled face with fierce black eyes, like a Goya portrait come to life. *'Con su permiso, señor.'* She apparently thought she should take over the task of applying the ice-cloth, but Gerardo was shaking his head firmly and he held out his hand for it.

'No, démelo, por favor!'

The cold cloth was handed over, but the small black eyes still peered over his shoulder while he pressed the coolness to Charlotte's brow, and she closed her eyes again briefly at the relief it brought. The frank curiosity in that wrinkled old face did not concern her at the moment.

68

'Does that feel better?'

The unmistakable voice aroused her once more, and she opened her eyes to find him still there. 'A—a little, thank you.'

Slowly the facts came back to her, though her brain still seemed curiously reluctant to function as she tried to remember. She had lost control when she hit a bump in the road, she could recall that much, but after that things were very much more confused. Having that composed but still slightly anxious face still hovering over her did not help her to think clearly either.

He wore no jacket and his silk shirt was thin enough to show the deep gold of his body through its texture; open at the neck to expose a strong brown throat. The bare arms looked powerful and she remembered how she had been carried all the way along that shadowy road from the gates. Gerardo Cortez was always a stunningly disturbing man, but never more so than now, and she was in no condition to cope with the effect of him on her dazed senses.

'What—what happened?'

Her voice was scarcely recognisable, even to herself, and her throat felt horribly dry and tight. His mouth twitched briefly into a ghost of a smile, but the black eyes were intent on what he was doing while he held the icy pad against her forehead.

'I can only assume that you once more lost control of that machine you ride with such panache,' he told her, and she noticed somewhat vaguely how he omitted any kind of a name when he addressed her. 'My *criado* found you near the gateway and ran back to inform me that you were unconscious and might be seriously hurt.'

'And you brought me back here?'

'*Sí*—I brought you back here, of course.'

Charlotte looked around her at as much of the room as she could see. Mostly her view was blocked by the high back of what appeared to be a settee of some kind, although it was bigger than any she had seen before, and by the tall figure that sat close beside her.

The huge beamed ceiling overhead would have been clue enough, but there were glimpses of walls too, that were hung with portraits and banners, and some fearsome-looking weapons. She vaguely recalled once vowing that she would never go walking into this particular spider's web, and yet here she was, not only in that huge fortress-like castle of the Cortez, but unable at the moment to do anything about getting out again.

She brought her gaze back to the man who bent over her so solicitously, and her heart was pounding wildly when she recalled once more the sensation of being carried in his arms. Of the softness of silk against her cheek and the warmth of a human body beneath it. Her lips felt suddenly dry and she moistened them with the tip of her tongue.

'I—I'm not seriously hurt, am I?'

He did not answer at once, but lifted the cloth from her brow and leaned forward to look more closely at the bump on her head, a movement that brought the lean warmth of his body still closer, until his broad chest just lightly touched her. The contact set her pulses racing so fast that she scarcely heard what answer he gave her.

'I am not a doctor, Señorita Grey, but I do not think you have anything more serious than a slight concussion. I have sent for Doctor Lopez, however, and it is he who will give the final verdict, of course.'

The use of her full name sounded very formal in the present circumstances, especially when she had distinctly heard him call her Charlotte just before she opened her eyes. Carefully she brought her mind back to more immediate things, like the fact that he had called a doctor.

'You've sent for Doctor Lopez?'

'But of course—it is he who must decide whether or not you are to go to the hospital.'

It was all happening much too fast, and she hastened to protest that she did not need even a doctor's attention, let alone to be taken to the hospital. 'Oh, but I'm not bad enough to have to——' While she made her protest she attempted to sit up at the same time, but a sudden sharp pain in her head brought on an unexpected wave of nausea and a swimming sensation that made her reach out and cling to the nearest solid support.

Her head was spinning so much that she closed her eyes and rested her forehead against his shoulder in sudden helplessness, while he held her by her arms, his face resting on the softness of her hair. His voice was deep and velvet soft close to her ear, '*Tranguila, pequeña!* Take care how you move!'

Charlotte gave her spinning head a moment to clear, then she raised it cautiously and looked at him through her lashes, her eyes narrowed against the throbbing ache across her brow. His mouth was touched by a hint of smile that showed too in the depth of the black eyes.

'You are too anxious,' he teased gently. 'Are you so nervous of being here that you cannot wait until you are fit enough to leave?'

Charlotte did not answer, but her tongue flicked once more across her dry lips, and she shifted her gaze almost anxiously when the wrinkled face of the old woman appeared once more beyond his shoulder. She held a glass of water in one thin hand which she handed to him. 'Señor—un poco agua.'

'Ah, gracias, María!' He took the glass from the old woman and held it to Charlotte's lips. 'Try a little water, as María suggests, but not too much.' An arm about her shoulders helped to support her and he held the glass still while she drank from it, the lukewarm water making her shudder at first. It would have been so much more refreshing if it had been really cold, but at least it slaked her thirst, and he took it away before she had taken more than a couple of mouthfuls. 'Is that better?'

'Yes—yes, thank you.'

He handed the glass back to the old woman and eased Charlotte away from him until he held her at arm's length, the black eyes searching narrowly over her face. 'It is better that you do not have too much to drink until we know more about this injury to your head,' he told her. 'How do you feel now?'

There was something slightly unreal about the situation, Charlotte thought hazily, but despite her throbbing head, the thought of having so much of Gerardo Cortez' time, of being the sole object of such tender concern, was not unpleasant. It was not of her own choosing that she was there, but he could easily have driven her to the Casa Berganza for Martha to take care of. The fact that he hadn't made her wish she felt better able to appreciate having gained a glimpse inside the castle, instead of feeling so achy and light-headed.

'I—I don't feel very——' She swallowed hard and allowed herself to be laid carefully back against the softness of the cushions again, while he watched her anxiously. 'I feel very peculiar,' she confessed.

'You must lie there and rest until Doctor Lopez has been to see you,' he told her, and once again she was struck by his gentleness.

She had seen him only as fierce and autocratic, and this new side to his character was a revelation that disarmed her completely. It was hard to think clearly and sensibly in the present situation, and her confusion was not entirely due to the bang on the head, she knew. Looking up at him where he sat on the edge of the settee, she knew that Gerardo Cortez had quite a lot to do with it.

'I'm being an awful nuisance to you,' she ventured, her voice dry and husky, and Gerardo shook his head.

'Do you wish me to agree with you?' He was smiling, and she found the effect of it unexpectedly disturbing, like the touch of him as he sat beside her. 'You must not talk,' he went on, giving her no time to reply. 'You must be very quiet until Doctor Lopez has decided what is to be done with you, so do not try anything foolish, hmm?'

It occurred to her suddenly that by now Martha might have started to wonder why she was not back from her ride, and she looked up at him anxiously. 'I —I think Aunt Martha—Señora Berganza, might begin to wonder where I am soon,' she said. 'If you could——'

'The *señora* is your aunt?' He seemed not to have taken note of the rest of her words, and she blinked at him a little vaguely for a moment before she replied.

'Not actually my aunt,' she told him, wondering why it mattered. 'She's an old school friend of my mother's and I call her aunt, it's a—a courtesy title.'

'Ah, so Luis Berganza is *not* your cousin?'

In normal circumstances Charlotte would undoubt-

73

edly have questioned his right to ask such personal questions—now she simply answered him with only a trace of a frown as she looked up at him.

'No, he isn't.'

He seemed to ponder on the information for a moment, then he nodded curtly and got to his feet, standing for a moment to look down at her. 'I will telephone Señora Berganza at once,' he promised. 'I shall tell her that you have had a slight accident but that there is no need for her to worry, the doctor is coming and in the meantime you are in good hands.' A black brow arched quizzically and a hint of smile showed on his mouth for a moment. 'You would agree with that, *señorita*?' he asked, and Charlotte nodded, noting the formality of that *señorita* with unexpected regret.

'Yes, of course,' she said.

'*Muy bien!*'

He turned and was gone in a matter of seconds, leaving her with only the old woman, María, for company in that huge raftered room. She made another attempt to raise herself and was much more successful this time. Her head throbbed, but she experienced none of the nausea or dizziness as she had in the first instance.

The ancient María, however, was beside her in a moment, her wrinkled face puckered anxiously as she reached out to help her, shaking her head. '*Cuidado, señorita!*' she warned, and Charlotte tried to smile at her reassuringly.

'I'm all right this time,' she told her, unsure if the woman knew any English or not. Her brain felt much too confused to cope with Spanish at the moment. 'I feel quite a bit better.'

74

Obviously she was understood, for the old woman was nodding and her almost toothless mouth smiled, creasing the wrinkled face still more. '*Bueno,*' she murmured. '*Muy bien.*'

She appeared almost to be standing guard, Charlotte thought, but it was not really necessary, for she did not feel in the least like doing anything more strenuous than sitting upright and looking around the room. Definitely she could not have tackled the walk from there to the Casa Berganza even had her present host allowed her to leave. She could hear his voice, quite some distance away, by way of an open door, and the vastness of the Castillo Cortez dawned on her more vividly when she caught a glimpse of some kind of huge hall beyond.

The room she was in was as comfortable as such a room could be, but its very size precluded any suggestion of cosiness. For all that it was homely, which was something that surprised her for some reason; perhaps because she had never seen Gerardo Cortez as a homely type of man.

The furniture was obviously very old and very heavy, in gleaming dark wood that glowed from centuries of good care, and the chairs as well as the huge settee on which she sat had high carved backs, and were upholstered with tapestry of some kind in red, gold and grey.

The ceiling beams were intricately placed, arching overhead into a mass of shadows, and were black, ornamented with gilt, while wide Moorish arches led out into a cool inner courtyard, a huge walled *patio* with gardens and fountains, lush beyond belief in such a setting. It was a beauty that the grim outside appear-

75

ance of the castle gave not a hint of, and she found it enchanting.

The room was impressive, almost regal, but it had an unexpected tranquillity too, a quiet coolness that was infinitely restful. She did not get up, but looked about her with such obvious interest that when the old woman caught her eyes she nodded, as if she understood her reaction.

'It's a beautiful room,' Charlotte said, and began to struggle with a Spanish translation, but María forestalled her.

'Is beautiful, certainly,' she agreed, and beamed a wrinkled smile that enjoyed her obvious surprise. 'Here are many such rooms, *señorita*.'

'I'm sure there are.' Her throbbing head was pushed to the background for the moment by her interest in the castle. 'It looks so enormous from outside, there must be dozens of rooms.'

María was nodding and her small dark eyes were bright and shrewd in her incredibly wizened features. 'If the *señorita* should desire to see—perhaps *el amo* will permit,' she suggested in her curiously stilted English, and Charlotte's surprise was plain to see when she looked at her.

'Do you really think Don Gerardo would——'

'What is it that you wish me to permit, Señorita Grey?' He came further into the room and for a second Charlotte felt an inexplicable skip in the steady beat of her heart as he came across the room towards her. She was still seated on the settee, though she was now perched on the edge of it with her feet on the floor instead of lying back on the cushions as he had left her. 'Did I not advise you to rest until the arrival of Doctor Lopez?' he asked sternly, but a second later

76

answered his own question. 'But of course you do not take advice if it prevents you from doing as you wish, do you, *señorita*?'

Charlotte could not imagine what had happened in the few minutes he had taken to make the call to Martha, but she felt certain that something had happened, for his mood was quite changed. The gentle concern he had shown earlier was replaced by the more familiar arrogance, and it surprised her to realise just how much she regretted it.

She glanced briefly across at María before she spoke, although heaven knew why, except that María was probably more accustomed to such changes of mood and might understand the present one better than she did herself.

'I am still resting, Don Gerardo; as you see, I haven't moved from here.'

'Only to sit upright and converse with María, instead of lying quietly!' he retorted. 'Were you discussing the possibility of having to be driven home by me, *señorita*—of ways to avoid that perhaps? If so, there is no need to concern yourself; Señora Berganza has left me in little doubt that both she and her son will be relieved when you are rescued from my clutches!'

'Oh, I'm sure she didn't say that!'

To Charlotte it was incredible that Martha had allowed her feelings to show so plainly. It was quite possible that she felt exactly as he said, but not that she had been so tactless as to allow him to know it. And yet when Charlotte looked up at him and saw the firm set of his mouth, and the jet-hard glitter of his eyes, she knew that something of Martha's opinion must have been conveyed to him. Gerardo was furiously angry, and there was no other explanation.

'Some things have no need to be put into words, *señorita*!' His eyes blazed down at her, and he seemed to disregard the presence of María, who still hovered in the background, fulfilling her role of *duenna*. 'I am left in no doubt that Señora Berganza fears for your reputation and for the reaction of her son, while you remain under my roof!'

'Oh, but I'm sure you mis——'

'Were you not yourself discussing how you could leave, when I came into the room?' he demanded, ignoring her attempted denial, and Charlotte shook her head, a gesture she immediately regretted as she put a hand to her aching brow.

'No, I wasn't,' she denied, husky-voiced and anxious to convince him. 'As a matter of fact, I was asking María if she thought you'd let me see more of the castle.'

He darted a glance at María and his eyes narrowed suspiciously. 'I think you already know the answer to that, Señorita Grey. El Castillo Cortez is my home, it is not a tourist attraction, and I am quite sure that Señor Luis Berganza would not countenance my showing you over my home!'

It was much too soon after the knock on her head, Charlotte told herself, and she was not thinking as clearly or as quickly as usual. She frowned at him curiously as he stood at the end of the big settee. 'I may be a little slow,' she said, 'but I don't quite see what it would have to do with Luis.'

She saw the same slight curl on his lip that she had noticed when he berated one of his countrymen on her behalf, and his eyes between their thick black lashes scorned her professed ignorance. 'Ah, but you do not allow anything to interfere with your wish to do as you please, do you?' he asked. 'I recall that you told me,

78

you were free to come and go as you please, seemingly not even a *novio* is to be allowed to change that!'

Charlotte struggled with the translation, almost too breathless to protest. Heaven knew why he was taking whatever Martha had said so much to heart, but she could not cope with his autocratic intolerance in her present state, and she felt quite alarmingly tearful as she sat with her hands clasped together in her lap, knowing that María's small, curious eyes were on her.

'I—I believe *novio* means fiancé,' she guessed, and her voice quivered uncertainly. 'If—if it does, then you have the wrong idea, Don Gerardo. I—I don't——' She swallowed hard, but the persistent tears could not be held any longer and they began to roll dismally down her cheeks. Her head was aching and she did not remember ever feeling more miserable in her life before.

'*Sagrada Madre de Dios!*' The words fell softly from his lips and were barely above a whisper, then turning swiftly to María he spoke to her over his shoulder. '*Marchase, por favor*, María!'

The old woman hesitated for a second, obviously reluctant to abandon her part as chaperone, but her employer's black frown made up her mind for her and she turned at last and left the room, closing the door behind her. She was hardly out of the room before he dropped down beside Charlotte on the settee and the black eyes looked at her for a second, studying her in silence. She could not see his face clearly enough to judge his expression, but he reached out suddenly and pulled her slowly into his arms until she could bury her face against his chest.

'I did not wish to make you cry, *chica*.' His voice was muffled by her hair as he held her gently. 'I would not do that.'

79

'I know.' Her voice was muffled, partly by the breath that caught in her throat as she tried not to cry, but partly because her face was pressed once more to the soft silk shirt and to the warmth of golden skin beneath it.

'Then please do not cry, hmm?'

Charlotte did not answer, but kept her eyes closed and her hands and face pressed to the comfort of his chest, and after a few seconds he reached with one big hand to span the nape of her neck and her head, easing her away from him. Strong fingers were twined in the silky softness of her hair while he studied her face for a moment with such an intense scrutiny that it seemed to sear like a flame through her senses.

'Charlotte!'

His voice was throaty, almost harsh, and he stressed the second syllable of her name in the Spanish way, pronouncing the final 'e'. The dark head bent closer, bringing a blurred impression of glittering jet black eyes and a firm hard mouth to block her vision suddenly, while his arms enfolded her again, harder and tighter than before and crushing her close to the steely vigour of his body with an urgency that stirred her own senses to respond. A response she had no control over, that wanted him to kiss her as she had never been kissed before.

If her head still ached, she was too dazed to notice it, and long lashes half concealed her eyes as she lifted her face to him, her lips parted. But in the moment that his mouth touched hers, a light irresistible touch, full of promise, there were voices suddenly, speaking in rapid Spanish, and the arms around her eased her away slowly and reluctantly, it seemed, holding her for a moment before the strong hands pressed her back against the cushions.

Gerardo was frowning, his brows drawn into a straight black line for a second or two, and the hands that put her away from him trembled a little as if with a passion that was held forcibly in check. He did not look at her again, but got to his feet and stood waiting for the doctor to join them, as cool and autocratic as only he could be, while Charlotte shivered with reaction and found it much harder to appear controlled.

Her dazed eyes registered the arrival of a short stout man in a smart grey suit and dark glasses, as he walked across the room ahead of María, then she put her hands to her face and tried desperately to bring herself back to reality. The dizzying throb of her pulse was due less to the knock on her head than to that unexpected moment with Gerardo, she suspected, but she found it difficult to bring her mind to bear on the basic practicalities the doctor needed to know.

'Señorita?' A cool professional hand took her wrist, and she put down her hands, but carefully avoided looking at Gerardo. 'You are the guest of Señora Berganza, are you not, señorita?'

An absent smile recognised her as having been in attendance when Martha had suffered from an upset stomach a few weeks before, and she remembered him as a pleasantly efficient man. 'I work for Señora Berganza,' she told him in a small and dismayingly unsteady voice, and the doctor nodded.

'You are in the habit of riding a bicycle, I understand.'

'Yes, but I—I'm always careful—I mean, the accident wasn't caused through my carelessness—not really.'

'Huh-huh!' He was too busy with what he was doing

to be entirely interested in what she was saying. 'A distraction, no doubt?' he suggested, and Charlotte did not bother to deny it.

He seemed satisfied with her pulse, and gave his attention to the bump on her forehead, asking short relevant questions while he did so. María stayed close, she noticed, but Gerardo went somewhere out of her range of vision, probably over by the window; she knew he was still in the room and it startled her to realise just how aware of him she must be to be so sure of that.

'I do not think there is much to worry about.' Doctor Lopez smiled at her reassuringly. He was coolly professional and much more fluently English than most people she had met in Spain so far, and he inspired confidence. 'You have been very fortunate, Señorita Grey, it will not be necessary to admit you to hospital. You must have rest and quiet, however, and preferably spend some of the next day or two in bed—but I have no doubt that Señora Berganza will see that you are well taken care of, hmm?'

'Oh yes, of course, doctor, but——' She hesitated, unwilling to admit herself ready to stay in bed even for a day. 'Is it necessary for me to stay in bed? I mean——'

From somewhere across the room Gerardo's deep, soft and unmistakable voice interrupted, saying something in his own tongue which made the doctor's brows raise curiously, and brought a hint of a smile to his mouth, so that Charlotte had little difficulty in guessing what the gist of that remark was, even without the aid of her little knowledge of Spanish.

'If the *señorita* is really so averse to being advised,' Doctor Lopez observed with a hint of humour, 'then perhaps I should relay my advice to Señora Berganza, who I am sure will see that it is followed.'

'There's no need!' Charlotte looked at him reproachfully, resisting the temptation to seek out Gerardo. 'I'm not foolish enough to deliberately make myself ill out of sheer pig-headedness, Doctor Lopez, no matter what Don Gerardo might suggest. If you think I should rest, then of course I will, though I feel much better already.'

'I am pleased to hear it!' The doctor closed his bag with a businesslike snap and smiled down at her. 'Now, if you will excuse me, Señorita Grey, I have another patient to see. I will call on you in two days' time, to make certain of your recovery. If you should need me in the meantime——'

'Yes. Yes, of course, thank you.'

It was María who saw the doctor out while Charlotte sat with her hands in her lap still, uncertain what to do or say next. If Gerardo were to say he would take her home she was ready to go willingly, but according to what he said earlier, Luis was coming for her. The big room seemed curiously still after the doctor's departure, but far from tranquil, for Charlotte could sense a certain tension in the air. It could stem only from the man behind her and she felt curiously on edge as she waited for heaven knew what to happen.

'Will you allow me to drive you home?'

He did not move, but spoke from where he stood, over near the window, and she did not turn round to look at him yet. 'If—if you will, please.' When she looked down at her hands she noticed how tightly clasped they were, and made a conscious effort to ease them apart.

His tread made no sound on the thick carpet as he

strode across towards her, and she looked up, almost startled, when he appeared beside her suddenly. She took the hand he offered, and got to her feet, but her heart was racing when his strong hard fingers closed over hers. They turned as one when voices reached them once more via the partly open door, and after a second or two Charlotte looked up at him with her eyes wide and anxious.

'Luis Berganza,' Gerardo said softly. 'Of course he would waste no time in coming for you!'

She clung to his hand, almost afraid to let go of it, and she shook her head, though with little idea of what it was she sought to deny. 'Gerardo, I——'

'But of course you will go with him, *chica.*' His voice was low and velvet-soft, and it shivered over her skin like a caress. 'He is right for you, you will see. Young and handsome and working at a worthwhile career—what more is there for you to ask?'

'Love!' Charlotte said, desperately seeking to convince him, and he smiled.

It was little more than a sardonic twist of his mouth that was echoed by the jet-black glitter of his eyes while he took her hand in his, but the brief warm pressure of his mouth in her palm made her catch her breath. 'A myth, Charlotte, a pretty myth.'

'*No,* Gerardo!'

The door opened wider to admit María, her wrinkled crone features discreetly expressionless, but by the time Luis appeared behind her there was a good two or three feet between Charlotte and Gerardo, and Luis noted the fact with narrowed dark eyes. Before they left, Gerardo took her hand again, but did no more than shake it politely. His black eyes were evasive and his hard fingers cool and merely polite in their presence, as if they were complete strangers.

'*Adiós, señorita,*' he said.

CHAPTER FIVE

IT was more than two weeks since the accident with her bicycle, and Charlotte was quite recovered, although at times she felt that the outcome of the incident had been curiously unsatisfactory. Of course she had not expected anything serious to develop between herself and Gerardo Cortez, but those few moments when he had touched her mouth with that disturbing promise of a kiss, had left her with a strange sense of restlessness that she could find no logical reason for.

She had not seen him since, except on a couple of occasions when she walked down to the village and he had driven past in his car. The first time he had slowed down sufficiently to call out and ask if she was recovered, but the second time he had done no more than acknowledge her with a casual half salute, and yet somehow each time she went out she found herself looking out for him.

It came as a welcome surprise when Luis asked her one evening if she would like to go to a party with him, and she accepted without hesitation. She loved the peace and quiet of San Cristóbal, but it would be nice for a change to look forward to something a little more exciting than her usual quiet life. Also there was the chance that it might appease that disturbing restlessness that plagued her.

It was Luis's apparent lack of enthusiasm for the party that puzzled her, and she looked across at him curiously as she questioned it. 'I thought you liked parties,' she said, and he pulled a wry face.

'Of course I like parties,' he told her, 'but not this sort so much. I like to think that I have nothing to do but enjoy myself, but in this instance I am expected to be polite to possible clients, and to one in particular, who could put a great deal of business our way.'

'You mean you're canvassing for clients?' She laughed at his rueful face. 'I thought lawyers didn't advertise!'

However lighthearted she had meant to seem it was clear from Luis's reaction that he took the matter more seriously. It was surely a pleasant and discreet way of sounding out new business, she would have thought, and she saw no wrong in teasing him about it, but Luis was obviously offended, and when he was offended he always looked so very Spanish that sometimes it startled her.

His head was angled in that stiffly proud way that characterised those portraits of bullfighters on the posters, or the arrogance of the male flamenco dancer. His chin was high and he looked down the length of a handsomely autocratic nose at her.

'I don't consider it advertising,' he denied sternly. 'It is simply that one is required to be polite to certain people who might at some time have need of our services. It is not the same thing at all as advertising, Charlotte.'

She should have known better, Charlotte thought, and glanced briefly and ruefully at his mother before she answered. 'No, of course it isn't, Luis—I'm sorry.'

He was as volatile as a weather-vane and he was contrite in a moment when she apologised. Under his mother's benign eye he reached across the table and squeezed her hand. 'Oh no, please do not apologise to me, dear Charlotte, I did not mean that you should. I suppose I'm just rather touchy on this particular subject because I'm required to be polite, even friendly, to a man whom I both dislike and distrust.'

Charlotte freed her hand as best she could without appearing too obvious, then she looked across at him and smiled as she got on with her meal once more. 'It doesn't sound like very much fun,' she remarked.

'Oh, but I am sure it will be!' He was anxious now to convince her for fear she changed her mind, she thought. 'You will enjoy it I'm sure, Charlotte.'

Willing to be appeased, she smiled at him curiously. 'Who is this ogre you have to be nice to?' she asked. 'Perhaps I can help a little by being charming to him!'

The remark had been meant as a joke, but it was clear that once more she had misjudged Luis's sense of humour. He was frowning darkly while he speared a strip of *churro* with his fork and swirled the pancake around in the chocolate sauce on his plate, and his voice was hard and flat. 'You will do nothing of the kind,' he declared firmly. 'I will handle Don Gerardo Cortez in my own way!'

For a second it seemed to Charlotte that she had stopped breathing. Gerardo Cortez had been on her mind so often during the past two weeks, but just for a while, while she was talking to Luis, he had been pushed to the back of her mind. Having his name brought so suddenly and so unexpectedly into their conversation startled her so much that for a second or two she could not think clearly.

'It—it's Don Gerardo that you're hoping to persuade to become a client?' she ventured, and hoped the slightly breathless quality of her voice was not too apparent.

Luis nodded, disposing of the mouthful of *churro* before he spoke. 'There's a great deal of legal business connected with a firm the size of that he controls,' he told her, 'and the old fellow who's been handling it died recently. Don Agustin hopes that at least a little of it will come our way.' He distorted his good-looking features with a grimace. 'What Don Agustin does not know is that I am not on such friendly terms with our illustrious neighbour as he thinks—personally I would as soon do business with a boa-constrictor!'

'You really dislike him so much?'

His reaction was startling, although she had had plenty of indications that Luis disliked the older man. The fact that he was watching her across the table, narrow-eyed, made her wonder if he could actually hear the thudding beat of her heart, and if he realised just how much the very mention of Gerardo Cortez had stirred her senses. From his answer it was plain that he at least suspected it.

'I dislike him because I am sure you do not, *mi amante*—I think you know that.'

Charlotte said nothing for the moment, but did her best to appear composed and got on with her meal, leaving it to Martha to chide her son. Leaning towards him, she touched his hand lightly, almost warningly it seemed, despite the quietness of her voice.

'Luis,' she said, 'I wish you wouldn't be so provoking, darling.'

Luis did not take his eyes off Charlotte, but watched her slightly flushed face with unnerving steadiness, noting the way her lashes concealed her eyes from him. 'Charlotte asked me a question, Mamá, and I answered her; I think you will find it makes no difference to her anticipation because she now knows Don Gerardo will be at the party—rather the reverse, I think. Am I not right, Charlotte?' He reached out and his fingers closed firmly around her wrist, his voice pitched in a much lower register than usual and edged with hardness. '*Am* I not right, Charlotte?'

Feeling rather as if she had been cornered, Charlotte said nothing about the hold on her wrist for a moment. It was a difficult situation, for Luis was the son of her employer, even though the relationship between her and Martha Berganza was hardly the usual one between employer and secretary.

In more usual circumstances she would probably have shaken him off and objected indignantly to the way he was behaving, but in the circumstances it was difficult to know just what to do or say. The tension in the air was disturbing, and yet somehow exciting too, and she had the unshakable feeling that somehow things between herself and Luis were on the brink of change—one way or the other.

'What do you want me to say, Luis?' She looked across at him as coolly as she knew how. 'You asked me to this party knowing I'd be bound to see Don Gerardo again, since you've implied you have to spend at least some of the time buttering him up for the business he can put your way. What do you want me to do? Say that I won't come now that I know he's going to be there? If that's so, Luis, why did you ask me in the first place?'

He resented the reference to his buttering up anyone, she could see that, it offended his pride, and his handsome face was flushed as he looked across at her. He made no more pretence of eating, but sat with his

89

hands together in front of his face, watching her closely.

'I wanted to think that it would make no difference to you whether or not he was there,' he told her in a voice that shook with the depth of his emotions, 'but I know that isn't possible, Charlotte. Therefore I can only hope that at least you will not be so—so distracted by him that you forget I am there! Not even for Don Agustin's benefit would I let you desert me for him without making my protest!'

Charlotte swept her glance swiftly over his face and met the burning intensity that gleamed in his eyes. This was a side of Luis that she had never seen before, and it made her uneasy. She had speculated on the possibility of his being a jealous lover in the event of their relationship becoming more serious, but the depth of passion he now revealed was even more intense than she had anticipated. Neither was Martha altogether happy about the present situation, she thought, although so far she had made almost no attempt to intervene.

'Naturally if I go with you,' Charlotte told him in a voice as cool and steady as she could make it in the circumstances, 'I shall stay with you, Luis. Good manners haven't deteriorated to that extent, even in decadent England!'

She realised how much her hands were trembling only when she put down her fork, and it startled her to realise how close they were to quarrelling. Martha too must have recognised the danger signs, for she looked from one to the other, then stepped in swiftly with the cool voice of reason, smiling determinedly.

'If you're going to a party, my dear,' she told Charlotte, 'you must have a new dress. Something very lavish and very expensive—I shall insist on choosing it myself as a present from me.'

'Oh no, Aunt Martha, I couldn't let you do that!' Charlotte welcomed her intervention, but she would prefer to buy her own dress. Not to do so would, she felt, put her standing with Martha on a slightly different footing, and she was wary of doing that at the moment. 'I will have a new dress, though—something soft and sexy.' She laughed a little unsteadily and did not look at Luis yet. 'It's time I dressed up again!'

'For my benefit?'

She looked across at Luis and caught a deep dark look in his eyes that sent a little shiver through her, but she had no time to answer before he reached again for her hand and held her fingers tightly. She would have freed herself, but to do so now, she felt, would give him quite the wrong impression, and she was suddenly much more wary of Luis.

'Naturally for your benefit, Luis,' she told him quietly. 'You want me to look nice for this party, don't you?'

He held her gaze determinedly for a moment, then raised her fingers to his lips. 'You always look nice to me, *mi amante*,' he murmured, and Charlotte glanced swiftly at Martha Berganza, seeing the small benign smile that touched her mouth.

'Isn't it your birthday that day, Charlotte dear?' she asked, as if the thought had only just come to her, and Charlotte nodded.

'Yes, it is, Aunt Martha.'

'Good!' Martha nodded, glancing with unmistakable meaning at her son. 'Then I shall get you a dress for your birthday present, my dear, and you cannot deny me!'

Luis still held on to her hand, and he searched her face with his dark eyes for a moment, half-smiling, then raised her fingers once more to his lips. 'I shall make it a birthday to remember,' he promised.

The postman did not deliver as he did at home, and for the first time since her arrival Charlotte missed the custom of opening her post at the breakfast table, as she would have been doing in England on her birthday.

She knew there would be cards and presents from home, but they would have to be opened later. For the moment there were two packages beside her place at the table. The dress Martha had insisted on buying for her, she had already seen when she tried it on, but she had no idea what could be in the small square gift-wrapped package from Luis.

Martha kissed her and hugged her affectionately, as if she suspected she was feeling slightly homesick. 'Happy birthday, my dear!' she said, and scanned her face briefly while she held her hands for a moment. 'I do hope you won't feel too—cut off from your family, having your birthday in a foreign land. I know you are rather a close-knit family and you must miss them, more especially at times like family celebrations.'

'Like you did, Aunt Martha?' The friendly grey eyes smiled and and she nodded.

'Just at first, my dear, not for very long.'

Charlotte returned her hug and smiled at her reassuringly. 'Don't worry about me, Aunt Martha, I feel absolutely at home here now, thanks to you—and to Luis, of course.'

'Especially to Luis, I think,' Martha insisted. She watched Charlotte smilingly while she opened up the box containing the dress she had bought for her and carefully lifted out the folds of bright blue silk. 'You'll look beautiful in that dress, dear,' she told her, 'and Luis will be so proud of you he'll want to show you to all and sundry!'

Holding it against her, Charlotte stroked the soft material with an almost sensual pleasure. 'It's gorgeous,' she said, unable to resist it even though she was still doubtful about the cost of it. 'But you were much too generous, Aunt Martha.'

'Oh, nonsense, child!' Martha's smile was indulgent, and it was plain from the look in her eyes what was going on in her mind. 'I feel that you're almost part of the family now, and anyway, I love buying dresses that I'm too old to wear myself!'

Charlotte folded the dress carefully back into its box, still stroking its softness as if the touch of it was irresistible. 'It's the most beautiful dress I ever owned,' she confessed. 'Thank you, Aunt Martha.'

Martha nodded, obviously well satisfied with the success of her gift, then turned swiftly with a smile when Luis came in to join them, sleek and handsome and smelling of after-shave. Martha adored her son, and never made any attempt to conceal it. Since seeing photographs of Luis's swarthily good-looking father, Charlotte found her devotion more understandable, for Martha had loved her husband deeply and Luis was exactly like him.

'Hello, darling.' She held out a hand to him. 'How are you this morning?'

'Good morning, Mamá.'

Luis kissed her as he always did, but his eyes were on Charlotte and his mother smiled her understanding, hugging him briefly before she let him go and picking up a newspaper as if she had no further interest in the proceedings, which was far from the truth, as Charlotte well knew.

He looked across and saw that the package beside Charlotte's place was still unopened and, after a brief shrug, he leaned across and picked it up, glancing from one to the other as he did so. 'Forgotten?' he queried softly, but with a smile that showed he did not for a minute believe it, and Charlotte hastened to deny it.

'Oh no, of course not, Luis!'

She watched him curiously when he walked across the room to gaze out of a window at the garden, cool in the morning breeze, with the package still in his hand, and when he turned suddenly and smiled an invitation to join him, she hesitated. She felt edgily uncertain for some reason she could not quite determine, and wary of him, though she did her best not to let it show as she walked over to join him in the window.

'Charlotte!' He put the gift-wrapped packet into her unresisting hands, then drew her in to his arms and held her for a moment while he looked down into her face. 'A very happy birthday, *mi amante*,' he murmured, and vaguely at the back of her mind Charlotte registered an objection to his more frequent use of that rather intimate endearment lately.

'Thank you, Luis.'

His eyes gleamed, bright and glowing, when he looked at her, and he indicated the parcel with a hint of impatience. 'Will you not open your present?' he asked. 'I am anxious to know if you like what I have chosen for you—I do so hope that you do.'

Charlotte freed herself from his arms and pulled off the wrapping paper with trembling fingers. A flat leather box with the name of an Arcos jeweller in gilt across the lid gave her a clue to the nature of the gift, and her heart was thudding in anticipation as she pulled off the last of the wrapping paper, for an expensive present of jewellery would put her in an equivocal position if she accepted it.

Even before the lid was more than half open she realised that her fears had been well founded. Her senses were stunned, not only by the diamond-studded bracelet that sparkled up at her, but the need to find the right words to refuse it. It was beautiful, but it would have cost far more than a friend would normally spend on a birthday gift, and if she accepted it she would be committing herself to something more than she was prepared to at the moment.

In the silence of the big room, her heart sounded like the beat of a drum as she stood there, anxious and indecisive. Martha could not see them without turning in her chair, but Charlotte sensed her interest, and Luis's dark eyes were fixed on her expectantly, so that she felt everything depended upon her first reaction.

On its cushion of black velvet the bracelet burned like white fire, shot through with rainbow brilliance, and she licked her suddenly dry lips hastily before she closed the lid firmly and stood with the box in her hands for a second longer before she looked up at Luis.

'I—I can't take it, Luis, I'm sorry.'

Her voice sounded curiously harsh, and it shook as if she was about to cry. The bracelet was the most beautiful thing she had ever been given, but she pushed it towards him, determined not to weaken.

'You don't like it?'

He sounded as if he did not believe that was her reason, and she made no attempt to pretend that it was. 'Of course I like it, Luis, but—I can't possibly accept anything so obviously expensive.'

Luis's hands closed over hers, crushing her fingers over the leather case. 'But of course you *can*,' he insisted.

'No, Luis—I'm sorry.'

She sounded breathless, her voice barely above a whisper, and the hands enclosing hers crushed them even more tightly, while his dark eyes gleamed with such determination that she felt a sudden sense of helplessnesss, as if she had little option but to yield.

'Charlotte!'

His voice was softly chiding, but she shook her head without looking at him. 'Luis, I can't possibly take such a present—you must realise that.'

'Give it to me!'

He was not denied, it was obvious, for he took the bracelet from its velvet bed with an alarmingly careless finger and dropped the box on to the table beside him, and Charlotte watched dazedly while he put the circlet of gold and diamonds around her left wrist.

'Beautiful!' He pressed his mouth to the soft skin of her inner arm briefly. 'Wear it,' he whispered persuasively. 'It is a birthday present without strings attached, Charlotte, I promise. Wear it tonight!'

'Tonight?' She looked at him vaguely for a moment until she remembered. 'Oh yes—yes, of course, the party's tonight, isn't it?'

Luis drew her close again, and kissed her mouth slowly and persuasively, his arms tight around her, then he looked down at her with his glowing dark eyes and smiled. 'Every man in the room will envy me my lovely companion,' he whispered, and Charlotte's heart fluttered anxiously.

The man who came first into her own mind was Don

Gerardo Cortez, and he would know how unlikely it was that she could afford to buy diamond bracelets for herself. He would have a very good idea who had bought it for her, and although it should not matter if Gerardo Cortez put the wrong interpretation on her wearing it, somehow it did, and as yet she did not stop to ask herself why.

Charlotte spent a lot of time before she left her room, debating the wisdom of wearing the bracelet that Luis had given her, but eventually she had decided against it. If she once wore it in public, she felt, she would be committed to keeping it for good, and she was still doubtful about doing that, when it was so obviously meant to be more than simply a birthday present.

Luis objected strongly when she appeared without it, and even his mother had obviously expected her to be less adamant about taking it when it came to the point. Consequently the evening got off to a rather less light-hearted start than it might have done, although she still had high hopes of it.

In the circumstances it was probably as well that Luis remained unaware that her first instinct on arriving was to look around for a sign of Gerardo Cortez, and she hastily pulled herself up when she realised it herself. Even so, she found it impossible not to search among the crowd of dark Spanish faces for the familiar autocratic features of the man Luis had been instructed to seek out and be polite to, regardless of his personal feelings.

She was standing beside Luis and a couple of business acquaintances, trying not to become utterly bored by a purely technical conversation, when she caught sight of Gerardo suddenly. He was on the far side of the room, but for a moment the people around him had drifted away and left a clear space between them, and for a breathless second the black eyes held hers steadily.

He inclined his head in the briefest possible bow, and she felt her heart begin a loud insistent drumming in her breast. In one short glimpse she registered everything about him. The stunning darkness of those rather stern features in contrast to a dazzlingly white shirt, and the gleaming blackness of his eyes between their short thick lashes.

She had not expected him to be alone, but catching sight of the woman beside him, she caught her breath. She was so startling in her vividness that she came as something of a shock to Charlotte, though heaven knew what kind of a woman she had expected him to prefer.

From her colouring Charlotte guessed her to be Spanish. She was tall and well built, with blue-black hair cut so short that it was virtually cropped like a man's, and bright dark eyes whose size was emphasised by the generous but skilful use of make-up. She used them a lot too, mostly to send heavy-lidded and meaningful glances at her companion, and her wide, dark red mouth was smiling, as if she found everything to her satisfaction.

It was difficult to believe that she could dislike anyone with such fervour without even knowing them, but Charlotte felt an intense antagonism towards that bright, vivid creature with Gerardo as she turned back once more to try and interest herself in Luis's conversation.

The discussion, she discovered, had become even more profound and lapsed more and more often into

Spanish, so that it was almost without thinking that she began to drift towards the doors that opened into the gardens. She stood for a while, looking out to a walled *patio* and enjoying a cooling breeze, the half-finished drink in her hand quite forgotten.

From the doorway to the quiet *patio* and the scented gardens was only a step, and she did not consciously avoid the anxious glance that Luis sent after her because he was too involved to follow. It would be nice to have a few moments alone in the gardens, and Luis could manage perfectly well without her for a while.

The gardens were large and as exotic as Spanish gardens usually were, within the confines of the traditional *patio*. Orange and lemon trees in company with fringed palms enclosed the whole garden, and rustled softly in the light wind, and roses and carnations grew in profusion in borders, and tumbled over the rims of countless stone urns and pots, their scents and colours mingling with musky-leafed geraniums.

At the centre of it all a massive carved stone basin caught the water from a fountain that played like showers of silver in the moonlight, and it was towards the water that she was inevitably drawn. Putting down her half-empty glass on the ledge around the basin, she sat down on the same ledge and watched the shadows on the cool water. It was incredibly peaceful and quiet, with the noisy chatter of the party becoming no more than a murmur in the background, and she shut her eyes for a moment to appreciate it, only to be snatched swiftly back by a voice that came from just behind her.

'May I get you another drink, Señorita Grey?'

It was a voice that was all too familiar; that velvet-soft timbre with its suggestion of steel, and her heart was already hammering hard in her breast when she turned and looked up into the dark-shadowed face of Gerardo Cortez.

For a second or two he watched her with an unnerving steadiness that she found hard to bear, so that she hastily looked away, trying desperately to still that wild uncontrollable beat of her heart. When she recalled the events of their last meeting and the way he had held her in his arms to comfort her, the way he had sent away the old servant, María, so that he could be alone with her, his present way of addressing her seemed uncompromisingly formal.

With the intention of showing him that she already had a drink, she reached out for the glass that stood on the ledge just in front of her, but nervousness made her clumsy and instead her hand knocked the glass and its contents into the water where it sparkled up at her through the shimmering surface, almost mockingly.

It was a quite unconscious reaction when she immediately leant over and plunged her hand in to try and recover it, but in the moment she did so, strong fingers closed swiftly round her wrist and stayed her, and there was an unmistakable thread of laughter in his voice when he spoke.

'Please leave it, *pequeña*, do not take the chance of falling in yourself, merely to retrieve a wine glass—I am sure our host would not consider it worthwhile!'

Her face flushed, Charlotte thought she knew exactly what he was thinking. He must think her the most clumsy and hapless female he had ever had the misfortune to meet, for never had their paths crossed yet except as a direct result of some carelessness on her part. She felt a helpless sense of frustration as she sat with her fingertips dripping with water and wishing that just once she could meet him when she was cool and collected, and not behaving like a clumsy idiot.

It was such a surprise when he took her hand in his suddenly that she caught her breath, and a briefly arching brow noted the dramatic and audible response. Taking a handkerchief from his breast pocket, he began to dry her fingers carefully, while she watched him dazedly, hastily avoiding his eyes when he looked at her.

'Is that dry enough?'

The effect of his voice was like a cool wind over her skin, and she nodded. 'Yes—thank you.'

When he let go her arm she instinctively put her own hand to the spot where the warmth of his strong fingers still lingered on her soft skin. His being there was disturbing, and especially so when she remembered that Luis was not very far away, and that he had sworn not to take it lying down if she should leave him for Gerardo Cortez. At the time she had thought it so unlikely to happen that she had been indignant at his even suggesting it—now that it was actually happening she did not see what she could do about it.

Also there was that vividly dark woman to consider, the one she had seen with Gerardo. She too had given the impression that she was unlikely to take kindly to finding them together, and causing a scene was the last thing Charlotte wanted, but still she could not bring herself to even attempt to bring the meeting to an end.

'You must think I'm the clumsiest female alive,' she suggested, and the shaky sound of her voice dismayed her.

Nor did Gerardo seem in a hurry to go, no matter who might be waiting. He placed one foot on the low ledge of the pool beside her, and rested his elbow on his knee while he looked down at her with a faintly quizzical look in his eyes.

'Rather I would say that you are—accident-prone. Is that the right phrase?'

He knew perfectly well it was the right phrase, Charlotte thought, for there was nothing wrong with his English, it was impeccable. 'That's the right phrase,' she agreed, and heard herself laugh in a way that betrayed all too clearly how unsure of herself she felt. 'Though in my case I think you're being kind, Don Gerardo—you're too polite to say I'm clumsy.'

His laughter, unlike hers, showed no trace of uncertainty. It was soft and deep and somehow reassuring, and he was shaking his head slowly over her argument. 'No one who is so enchantingly lovely can be called clumsy, *pequeña*. I would say the truth is that there are occasions when you react a little too—over-anxiously, but that is the fault of circumstance.'

Charlotte's heart beat made her breathless and slightly light-headed, but she also felt strangely more confident suddenly, and when she smiled up at him the moon lent a glowing darkness to her blue eyes and softened the contours of her face to a shadowy mystery.

'That's a very gallant way of saying I'm clumsy!' she told him and when she laughed this time it had a deeper and more provocative sound.

Gerardo's black eyes seemed disturbingly close and they traversed her face slowly in a searching look that caused a curious curling sensation in her stomach. 'I do not believe I can be the first man to tell you how lovely you are.' Once more that silky-soft voice shivered along her spine, and he smiled. 'Am I, Charlotte?'

She found it impossible to look away and yet she

shook her head without quite knowing why. 'Don Gerardo——'

'And yet I found you alone in the moonlight,' he went on, just as if she had not spoken. 'Have you deserted Señor Berganza?'

He must have known that there was sufficient provocation in the question to bring a response from her, especially combined with the thread of laughter in his voice when he asked it, and she looked up at him with a hint of challenge in her eyes. 'Have you deserted *your*—friend, Don Gerardo?'

In the silence that followed her heart drummed wildly, fearing she might have angered him, for she would not have that for anything. Only a moment later, she looked up swiftly when the deep sound of his laughter startled her, and she caught the stark whiteness of his smile in the dark shadowy face.

'I had vowed that I would not come near you this evening,' he confessed with stunning candour, 'but when I saw you come out here alone I was——' Broad shoulders shrugged beneath the impeccably tailored jacket, and between their thick lashes his black eyes glowed darkly. 'I admit that I was tempted to follow you and I succumbed to the temptation as I had vowed not to. I wished to assure myself that you were fully recovered from your accident.'

She did not believe his reason, she thought dazedly, and she did not think he meant her to, but she answered him quite seriously and avoided his eyes as she did so. 'That—that was very kind of you, Don Gerardo.'

'Not at all Señorita Grey! Since you chose one of my gates on which to attempt to break your neck, the least I can do is to enquire after your health!'

The use of her full title, she realised, was a kind of mocking retaliation for her own formality, and she made mental note of the fact that as well as being arrogant and autocratic on occasion, and gentle when circumstances called for it, he had a sense of humour, though a somewhat mocking one, judging by her own experience.

It was rapidly becoming more difficult for her to remain even as self-possessed as she had been so far, and she held her hands tightly together in her lap while she looked down in to the water in the stone pool. Its surface was rumpled like silver grey silk where the fountain disturbed it, and it made an incredibly romantic setting in the scented moonlit gardens, but if Luis should take it into his head to come and look for her, she shuddered to think what the outcome would be. For sure there would be little hope of Gerardo's legal business going to Don Agustin's firm.

'I'm perfectly all right now, thank you.' She brought her mind hastily back to more immediate matters, but glanced instinctively in the direction of the brightly lit doorway of the house. 'I—I think I should go inside now, Don Gerardo—if you'll excuse me.'

Even now he made no move, and she somehow felt curiously reluctant to break away while he was still there. Instead he swept a slow and infinitely disturbing gaze over her slim rounded figure in the flattering softness of blue silk, and smiled.

'It was rather unwise of Luis Berganza to risk your being bored by bringing you to an affair like this,' he observed with remarkable coolness. 'His attention was bound to be required on matters of business, leaving him little time to dance attendance upon you.'

Charlotte felt her face colour as she got to her feet.

She was prepared to deny that she was bored, however true it was, for Luis's sake, and she disliked his suggestion that she expected anyone to be constantly in attendance. 'I don't expect anyone to—dance attendance on me, Don Gerardo!'

'No?' The black eyes let her know that he did not believe it and once more she flushed under their mocking scrutiny. 'But will you also deny that you were bored when you left the party to come out here, *pequeña*?'

That rather childish endearment was becoming increasingly disturbing, and she wished she was more sure that she wanted him to stop using it. 'I *was* a bit tired of trying to follow a purely business conversation that was mostly in Spanish,' she admitted, 'but I knew what kind of party it was when I accepted the invitation. We would have gone somewhere to celebrate tonight anyway, but since we couldn't go to a restaurant as we would have liked, I didn't mind coming here.'

'To celebrate?' His interest was apparent, and she answered him without hesitation.

'It's my birthday,' she told him.

'Today is your birthday?'

Her heart was beating hard and fast, though she was not quite sure why, and she nodded her head. 'I know it's different in Spain,' she said, 'you celebrate the day of your special saint rather than your own birthday, don't you?'

'That is so—but your custom is different, hmm?' She was so totally unprepared for what happened that she gasped audibly when he bent and brushed his lips lightly against her cheek, just beside her mouth. 'May you have many more happy birthdays, *pequeña*. *Mucho dicha!*'

His breath was warm on her cheek and there was no time at all to bring herself back to earth after the surprise of it, because Luis seemed suddenly to come striding out of nowhere. His handsome face was contorted with anger and his eyes blazed, and the words he said were in Spanish, flat and harsh and obviously virulent, but the thing that brought Charlotte's hands up to her mouth was the swinging fist that aimed at Gerardo's jaw.

It was with almost sickening relief that she realised anger made Luis clumsy and that Gerardo's reaction had been as swift as she remembered from her own first encounter with him. He stepped aside swiftly, avoiding the blow, then snatched at Luis's wrist with his hard strong fingers and held on, while Luis cursed him.

There was little to choose between the depth of their anger, she thought a little dazedly, but whereas Luis had behaved with hotheaded rashness, Gerardo was still icily controlled. He said nothing for the moment in reply to those virulent curses, but she recognised the same look of contempt in his eyes that she had seen for the man who had accosted her when she explored Arcos alone, and he retained his hold, even while Luis tried angrily to free himself from it.

His mouth had a tight cruel look and he discarded the wrist he held suddenly, as if he found the contact repellent, and Charlotte felt a thin shiver of sensation along her spine as she watched with breathless anxiety. When she put a hand on Luis's arm, it was meant as a warning, reminding him that he had a great deal to lose if he went on.

'Luis——'

He turned and looked at her, almost as if he had

only now realised she was still there, then Gerardo too looked at her and he inclined his head in one of those stiffly formal little bows, his heavy-lashed lids concealing the angry glitter in his eyes. He ignored Luis, and spoke to her alone, but with such formality that she felt a curious sense of regret after the intimacy of the last few minutes.

'I regret that you have been obliged to witness this—incident, Señorita Grey; it is in fact regrettable that it happened at all, but I hope you will not judge the manners of my country too harshly because of it.' The flat coolness of his voice put Luis in the wrong more thoroughly than a tirade of angry words could have done, and she felt his arm taut under her fingers. 'Please—excuse me if I leave you alone, but I do not think you have anything to fear.'

It was several seconds before Luis recovered sufficiently to realise in full the implication of those last few words, and by then Gerardo's tall, arrogant figure was more than half way across the *patio* and heading for the lighted doorway into the house. Luis had been given a lesson in manners that he would not easily forgive, and for some curious reason Charlotte could feel sorry for him. He was no match for Gerardo Cortez—although few men would be, she thought.

Her hand still on Luis's arm, she pressed her fingers lightly in to the taut muscles. 'Luis, I'm sorry that happened.'

It was a second or two before he turned and looked at her, and Charlotte did not remember ever seeing that particular expression in his eyes before. That he saw her as at least partly to blame for what had happened, was obvious, and she felt a sudden sense of apprehension when she looked at him. If he was angry enough, and vengeful enough, she thought Martha would send her home, however unwillingly.

'So you should be, *amante*,' he told her in a husky and slightly unsteady voice. He looked at her for a moment down the length of his handsome nose, that glitter of resentment still there in his eyes, and she realised how much it had hurt his pride to find her with Gerardo Cortez. 'It is unlikely that the Cortez legal business will come our way now—I hope you are satisfied!'

CHAPTER SIX

It was hurtful as well as unfair, Charlotte thought, that she should be held responsible for the possible loss to Don Agustin of some very important business. Her conversation with Gerardo Cortez might have been unwise in the circumstances, but there had been little she could have done to avoid it, and she was not ready to admit to any cause for Luis reacting the way he had.

It had been disturbing, too, that his mother seemed to share his opinion that it had been largely her fault he had failed in his task of acquiring Don Gerardo's business for his employer. Not that Martha's reaction should have surprised her, for anything that affected Luis or his career was very close to her heart, and she still could not understand why Charlotte did not jump at the chance of marrying her son.

It was logical that she found it hard to forgive any action likely to hinder his chances, but hurtful too. In Charlotte's case too, it seemed, insult had been added to injury by the fact that she had been caught flirting with Gerardo Cortez, when she had declared herself so firmly against any such action.

Flirting was Luis's word for the light and very chaste kiss that he had witnessed last night, but nothing Charlotte said would convince him of its innocence. After that, nothing seemed to go right, and they had left the party much earlier than they had originally planned and arrived home so obviously at odds with each other that Martha had noted it anxiously.

Charlotte would have liked nothing better than to have gone straight to her room and left any discussion until morning when tempers had cooled and they were both more rational, but Martha was anxious and Charlotte was hardly in a position to argue with her. To give him his due, Luis had taken quite a bit of persuading before he told her about the incident with Gerardo, but once launched on his narrative he had omitted nothing, either of what he had actually witnessed, which was negligible, or what he suspected.

He had caught her in the garden with Don Gerardo, he declared, and they were kissing. Denying it was no use because he had seen it for himself and he felt quite entitled to be angry and to take the action he had. He had regretted mentioning his rash attempt to hit out, Charlotte realised, but having said it he went on, and for the first time, Martha looked out of sympathy with him, though not for very long.

She could understand his anger, she said, and once more turned her reproachful eyes on Charlotte, trying to understand how she had found it in her heart to take such a step when she knew how it was bound to affect Luis. Nothing Charlotte offered in her own defence made any difference to their conviction, and indeed it seemed to her at one point that he was almost enjoying his moment of drama, although she dared not suggest it.

He gave every appearance of suffering and even admitted that he should have had more sense than to take her, knowing that Gerardo Cortez was going to be there as well, but he had trusted her word. With Martha believing every word of it, for the first time since her arrival in Spain, Charlotte felt at odds with the people around her.

She had gone to her room at last, feeling more than a little apprehensive about her future at the Casa Berganza, and for a while she even toyed with the idea of finding out whether or not the post that Gerardo Cortez had offered her was still open. The more she thought about it, the more confused she became and her sleep was restless and uneasy all night.

Breakfast the following morning, however, was no different to any other morning, except that the atmosphere was possibly a little more strained and conversation did not flow with its customary ease. No one snubbed her and she knew it had been foolish to suppose they would, but she was still in no doubt that they found her behaviour of last night, or Luis's version of it, hard to understand.

Immediately after breakfast Martha left them. Whether with the idea of encouraging a reconciliation or not, Charlotte had no idea, but as she rose from the table Luis got up too and came round to her, catching her hand in his and preventing her from leaving. His eyes as he searched her face for a moment before he spoke had a dark brooding look.

'What are you doing today?' he asked, and Charlotte shrugged uneasily, taken by surprise.

'I don't know exactly,' she told him, trying to remember the few definite tasks she had lined up for her. 'There are some letters to do, I know, and I think Aunt Martha wants me to make a dental appointment for her.' She looked up at him curiously, wondering if he meant to take a day off and suggest she spent it with him, or if there was some other reason behind his unaccustomed interest in her daily routine. 'Why, Luis?'

He was slow in answering, and that alone gave her some clue as to what was on his mind. Also he was avoiding her eyes instead of looking at her with his usual bold and slightly provocative gaze. 'I am interested, that's all,' he said.

'Interested?' Charlotte raised her chin and there was a glint of challenge in her blue eyes as she regarded him through her lashes. 'Or suspicious, Luis?'

It was a challenge she had known he could not resist, and she noted the way his head came up in that proud, defiant way he had, and the glitter in his eyes. 'With good reason, *amante*!'

'With *no* good reason!' Charlotte denied shortly, and shook herself free of his hand. 'And if you distrust me so much that you don't believe a word I say, then you shouldn't call me *amante*! Love to me means trusting!'

'It also means jealousy, Charlotte!' He came round to stand in front of her, and his hands gripped hers tightly as he held them to his chest, his fingers hard and urgent, stressing the fierce darkness in his eyes. 'Do you not realise how jealous I am of him, my darling? How can I bear to see you kissing him when you will not even wear my birthday present to you? Can you not understand how I feel—how I suffered last night?'

Charlotte's voice had a breathless, uncertain sound

and she did not look at him when she spoke but kept her eyes instead on the throbbing pulse in his throat that, more than anything else, showed the depth of his emotions. 'If only you'd believe me when I tell you the truth, Luis, you wouldn't need to feel as you do. I wasn't kissing Gerardo—Don Gerardo, he kissed me, lightly and on my cheek after I mentioned that it was my birthday, that's all.'

That slip over Gerardo's name was bound to have been noted, she thought ruefully, and waited for him to remark on it. 'You call him by his christian name?' he asked, his voice flat and harsh, and Charlotte shook her head, rueing her own carelessness.

'No, I don't—I call him Don Gerardo, just as you do, but it makes no difference what I call him, Luis, you have neither cause nor right to be jealous!'

'No right?' He looked taken aback for a moment, and his dark eyes scanned her face anxiously. 'But you know that I love you, Charlotte.'

It simply wasn't possible to make him understand without being more hurtful than she wanted to be, and when she looked up at him at last, the regret she felt showed plainly in her eyes. 'But I *don't* love you, Luis—I'm sorry, but I—I don't, and I won't lie to you about it.'

He had heard it before but, Charlotte realised, it had never really impressed itself upon his mind before, and he did not want to believe it even now. He looked at her for a moment, and she saw the disbelief, the suspicion that darkened his eyes.

'Because of him?' It was incredible how much anger and dislike he managed to put into those few simple words, and she shook her head hastily.

'No, of course it has nothing to do with Don Gerardo,' she told him. 'I scarcely know the man, Luis, and you saw what his taste in women is like at the party last night.' She remembered it all too well herself, she thought, and recalled the jet black hair and the vivid mouth and eyes of the dark woman who had gazed with such ardour at Gerardo Cortez. She laughed shortly and rather more bitterly than she realised. 'Dark, bold and brassy is Gerardo Cortez' passion evidently, and that leaves me well out of the running, doesn't it?'

Luis slid a hand under the silky softness of her hair and his palm was warm and smooth on her neck as he held her head firm. 'It tells me that his tastes include the bold and the brassy, my darling,' he said, 'it does not tell me yours.'

He noted the swift warm flush that coloured her cheeks when she pulled away from him, her chin in the air. 'I don't have any particular likes,' she informed him, breathlessly defiant, 'but I dislike being—pinned down on the subject of matters that only concern me, Luis!'

'Charlotte——'

'No, Luis, please!' She was trembling, far more affected by the scene than she had realised, and she shook her head as she put a hand to her hair and absently pushed it back from her face. 'I just don't want to become involved with anyone at the moment, and if you—if we can't agree, I feel that perhaps I ought to——' She bit off the words sharply, unwilling to suggest she left Martha's employ, although it might yet become inevitable if she could not put matters straight with Luis. 'I don't want to leave here, Luis, I don't want to leave Aunt Martha, but I don't know that I can stay on if you—if we can't straighten this out once and for all.'

She turned hastily from him when she saw the curiously desperate look in his eyes, and stood with her hands tight together, trying to still their trembling. Then he gripped her arms suddenly and turned her to face him, shaking his head in vague disbelief.

'You wouldn't,' he said, his voice barely above a whisper. 'You wouldn't go and work for him, Charlotte, would you?' Without giving her time to answer, he tightened his grip and she was pulled forcibly against him until she put up her hands between them, tightly curled into fists as she tried to resist. 'Charlotte, in God's name, tell me you won't go to him—that you won't move into that damned castle! You know it wouldn't stop at being his secretary, don't you? You know he wouldn't be content just to have you there and not—Oh, Charlotte, please promise me you won't work for him!'

Charlotte shook her head, unaware of the rather bitter smile that touched her mouth when she looked up at him. 'Do you imagine I'll be given another chance to?' she asked.

'Would you have gone?'

She met the challenge with a quivering uncertainty, for she had a suspicion deep in her heart that if the opportunity was offered to her again she would go and work for Gerardo Cortez without stopping to question other possible involvements. Instead of admitting it, however, she cast her eyes down and shook her head.

'No, of course not,' she said.

'Oh, Charlotte!' His voice was barely audible and he reached out to take her in his arms again—not forcefully this time, but with a gentleness that was curiously affecting, holding her close while he rested his chin on the top of her head, on the silky softness of her

114

hair. 'It was so hard for me, *amante*, to see you with him, but I begin to believe that you are telling me the truth about it.'

'I am,' Charlotte said. 'If you hadn't been so ready to believe the worst, Luis, it might have saved a lot of trouble for everyone.'

'And now you hate me!'

The dramatic statement was so typical of him that Charlotte found it impossible not to smile as she shook her head. 'Of course I don't hate you,' she denied. 'Why should I, Luis?'

'Oh, my sweet Charlotte!' He hugged her closer, so obviously relieved that their temporary disagreement was over. 'If I am patient,' he whispered,' who knows, perhaps you will change your mind about becoming —involved, huh?' He kissed her brow lightly, and she knew he was smiling from the sound of his voice. 'I'm sorry about making such a fuss, Charlotte—will you forgive me?'

She eased herself away from him and looked up at the handsome, confident face, wondering if he really had been convinced about her feelings after all. 'I forgive you,' she said, and gave an inward sigh of resignation. 'Now, hadn't you better start for the office before you're late?'

Luis pulled a face, his eyes clouded for a moment at the prospect of facing Don Agustin's questions regarding his success with Gerardo Cortez. 'I shall have to try and explain somehow about the Cortez business,' he said, 'but Don Agustin isn't going to be easy to convince that there is no hope of getting it now.'

'Will you tell what you—will you tell him everything?'

He made another grimace, though he was far more

concerned than he showed, she thought, and for the first time she felt a twinge of conscience about her part in his failure. 'I don't know.' He shrugged, and it was clear from his expression that he did not relish telling the full story. 'I shall perhaps simply tell him that— there was trouble between us and that it is unlikely Don Gerardo will be putting any business our way.'

'Won't he ask what *kind* of trouble?'

Luis's shrug and the resigned spread of his hands were very Spanish, and he smiled ruefully. 'Perhaps,' he admitted. 'If he does then I shall have to tell him something close to the truth but not the exact truth— I do not think he would understand the true reason for my doing what I did.'

'Luis.' She traced the outline of his jacket lapel with a finger tip and did not look at him. She had been about to suggest that she try and do something to help, but she had no feasible ideas at the moment, so that when he looked at her curiously, she shook her head and laughed. 'I'll try and think of something,' she promised vaguely. 'Now, for heaven's sake, Luis, go to work—you'll be late!'

He held her tightly for a moment and his eyes were bright and anxious. 'You forgive me?' he asked, and she nodded.

'Yes, of course I do.'

'*Gracias, amante!*'

He pulled her into his arms again and kissed her mouth with an ardour that took her breath away, but Charlotte protested only mildly, for her mind was suddenly made up. There was a way she could put things right for Luis, and she felt confident she would have the nerve to do it.

It had seemed like the perfect solution when Charlotte first thought about helping Luis by appealing directly to the man most concerned, but now that she was faced with the fact of doing it, suddenly she had a great many doubts. Gerardo Cortez was not an easy man to approach with a petition such as she had in mind, and after last night's episode he was unlikely to view any appeal on Luis's behalf with very much sympathy, but she felt she must try.

It had not been necessary to make a special journey to the village, because she had letters to post for Martha, so no one questioned her going out, and she was not obliged to manufacture excuses. When she left the post office and picked up her bicycle again, however, she hesitated for several seconds before she rode off in the direction of the castle, still unsure about the wisdom of going.

The sight of Padre Larraga crossing the square with a couple of his parishoners did nothing to strengthen her resolve either. He had reported seeing her drive off with Gerardo in his car, so his sense of propriety would surely be outraged at the idea of her calling on him in his home.

She acknowledged the old priest with a polite greeting, and hoped he was too involved with his duties to notice in which direction she was riding. Whether he did or not, it was too late to turn back now, and she cycled faster as she neared her objective so as to leave no time for last-minute panic.

Huge fig trees almost met across the narrow private road that sloped more steeply as it neared the castle, and the oleanders and magnolias that grew in their shade were lushly overgrown into a jungle of scented blossom. It seemed incongruous somehow to arrive at the front entrance of a castle on her bicycle, so she left it concealed behind one of the huge stone gateposts and set off on foot, brushing her hands nervously down her dress as she started.

There was a breathless silence under the shadowy darkness of the trees, and a coolness that sent little shivers through her as she left the road behind. It was all too easy to imagine the original Moorish Cortez, fierce, dark overlords of the whole valley, riding along this same route, and she felt her scalp prickling at the imagined sound of hooves and the snorting breath of impatient horses.

A bend in the road hid from her the distance she had already come, and she felt strangely isolated suddenly, as if she had been cut off from the rest of the world. Standing for a moment among the silent trees she listened to those curious and disturbing sounds, then shook herself hastily. Active as her imagination was in such influential circumstances, it soon became clear that the sound of hooves and the stertorous breathing of a horse being ridden hard was not a figment of her imagination, but a fact, and she stepped back a little to where she could see the rest of the road and the gates.

It took only a second for her to recognise the horseman, riding across from one side of the road to the other, as the man she had come to see, and her heart gave a swift, breathtaking lurch at the sight of him mounted on a shiny black Arab horse—exactly the kind of sleek beauty that must have carried his Moorish ancestors with such pride.

His broad back was to her so that she remained unseen as she watched from the concealment of the thick-growing shrubs, but the beat of her heart was fast and furious, and she felt a tingling sense of excitement. He looked as straight and arrogant as always and somehow even more impressive on horseback, and she shook her head over the effect he could have on her, as she watched him disappear into the trees beside the road.

When he was gone and the silence surrounded her again, she had to shake herself out of a curious kind of lethargy and resume her walk along the tree-lined approach. A churning excitement brought a flush of colour to her cheeks and it was disturbing to think that a man she scarcely knew could arouse such a violent reaction in her, and yet there seemed little or nothing she could do about it.

The craggy ramparts of the Castillo Cortez loomed before her with unexpected suddenness and she experienced another moment of doubt when she was faced with a pair of massive dark wood doors that were firmly closed and looked horribly discouraging. She retained no visual impression of the castle from this point, for the last time she had come she had been carried in to it, unconscious, in the arms of Gerardo Cortez. Nor had she taken much note when she left with Luis, some time later, for then her mind had been too preoccupied with the fascination of its owner to take much note of the castle itself.

It seemed huge and strangely menacing, looming about her as it did on three sides. Its foundations plunged downwards steeply into a mass of trees that completely hid the bottom regions of the castle and the rock on which it was built, and Charlotte could not restrain a sudden shiver as she reached for an iron bell-pull that hung beside one of the doors.

There was no deafening clanging of bells, as she expected, in fact she actually heard nothing, but it was only a matter of moments before one of the doors opened and she heaved an almost audible sigh of relief when she recognised the wrinkled brown face of the old woman who had helped tend her when she was hurt.

María appeared startled at first and stared at her as if she did not believe her own eyes, but then she inclined her head politely and stepped back to invite her in, her toothless mouth stretched in to a smile. '*Adelante, señorita, por favor;*' she said, but Charlotte hesitated for a second, doubtful again.

'Is it—is it all right if I come in?' She smiled a little uncertainly and shook her head. 'I mean I don't want to come if it isn't convenient.'

'Ah, *por favor, señorita, adelante!*'

Another toothless smile encouraged her and with a sudden decisive nod, she followed old María into the entrance hall. She had passed through it once before, when she was on her way home with Luis the last time she was here, but she had not been sufficiently aware then to notice it very much. Looking round her now she found it stunningly impressive.

It was so huge that it reminded her in some ways of the soaring vastness of a cathedral, though it was obvious from its style and decor that its inspiration had been the homeland of the Moorish lords who built it. It was huge and quite breathtakingly beautiful to Charlotte's bemused eyes, and she gazed around her as she followed María across its beautifully tiled floor.

A series of Moorish arches with slim marble pillars were gilded and painted and supported an upper floor for roughly two-thirds of the hall's depth, while those immediately inside the doors ascended directly into the shadows of a vaulted ceiling. At either side twin staircases curved upwards, their balustrades intricately decorated and leading to what appeared to be a long gallery which in turn carried more arches that were fretted and gilded where they overlooked the hall.

The whole effect was of one building inside another and it was like nothing Charlotte had ever seen before, so that she stopped and gazed around her without realising she was doing so until María brought her gently back to earth. 'I will see if Don Gerardo has returned, *señorita*.'

'I—I saw him coming along the road,' Charlotte told her, 'but he looked as if he might be on his way back.' She hesitated, still somewhat overawed by her surroundings, and knowing how curious María must be about her visit. 'I—do you suppose he'll see me for a few moments, María? It's rather important.'

'I am sure, *señorita*!' She seemed so certain and her small black eyes glistened in a way that suggested there was no doubt at all in her mind. Perhaps she was recalling the fact that the last time Charlotte was there, her employer had dismissed her so as to be in the room alone with the visitor, 'I will tell *el amo* that you wish to see him,' she told her. 'You will see, *señorita*!'

'María! *Qué pasa?*'

The voice from across the hall was imperious, demanding attention, but old María answered its summons only reluctantly, that was quite obvious, and Charlotte turned swiftly when she heard it. A tall, brown-haired woman was coming across the hall, her head high and with a brittle air of authority about her that suggested she had every right to question María's doings, and at the sight of her Charlotte felt a sudden coldness in her stomach. Until now it had not even occurred to her that Gerardo might have a guest staying in the castle, and to discover he had proved horribly embarrassing.

A pair of cool grey eyes swept over Charlotte from top to toe and there was no trace of a smile on the cool chiselled features. 'Good morning,' she said. 'May I help you?'

Before Charlotte could reply, María took the onus upon herself, speaking rapidly in her own tongue, watching the woman with her small black eyes. But whatever she said made no impression, it was obvious, and once more Charlotte became the target of those rather hard grey eyes.

'I heard María speaking to you in English, so I presume you're English,' she said. 'How may I help you, Miss——?'

'Grey,' Charlotte obliged. 'Charlotte Grey.'

She felt very inadequate suddenly and very out of place in her simple pink cotton dress and the inevitable white hat, while the woman who faced her looked cool and elegant in cream silk and high-heeled shoes that did a great deal more for her long slender legs than Charlotte's summery sandals did for hers. She resented the other woman's attitude, but to some extent she could understand it if she was indeed one of Gerardo's more intimate friends.

'I had rather hoped to see Don Gerardo,' she said.

Once more that cool and distinctly suspicious gaze swept over her and Charlotte mused on the amount of nerve it must take to behave with such authority in Gerardo Cortez' house, unless she was very sure of her position there.

'I'm afraid that won't be possible,' the cool distant voice informed her flatly. 'If you wish to see Don

Gerardo on a matter of business I could probably help you—I'm his secretary.'

So that was it! Charlotte almost laughed aloud, shaking her head over the quite incredible sense of relief she felt. The woman was nothing as intimate as a paramour after all, but simply someone filling the post that Gerardo had originally offered to her.

'I know Don Gerardo isn't here at the moment,' she said, feeling suddenly as if she had the advantage, although heaven knew why, 'I saw him on the road just now, but he's on his way back and I need not bother you if María tells him I'm here.'

She was taking a chance, she knew, but the glint in María's black eyes encouraged her, and she could guess that there was little love lost between them. Probably María had been with the Cortez for most of her life and resented the arrival of a domineering secretary. She did not wait further, but turned to go, presumably to do as Charlotte said, and inform her employer, but before she had taken more than a step, that sharp imperious voice pulled her up short.

'*Espere un momento!*'

María looked at her inquiringly, not as overawed as the other woman would have wished, Charlotte thought. '*Sí*, Señorita Fane?'

'There's no need to bother Don Gerardo,' the secretary told her, 'I am here to deal with things like this!' She turned her attention once more to Charlotte and her grey eyes had a hard icy look that defied anyone to override her authority. 'I'm afraid it isn't convenient for Don Gerardo to see anyone this morning,' she said, 'he's much too busy, Miss—Grey? If you'd care to leave a message I'll see that he gets it, or you could make an appointment through me—I'm afraid he has no time for casual callers.'

Heaven knew what got into her, but Charlotte was tempted, and she found the temptation irresistible. She widened her blue eyes to their widest and most guileless, and smiled. 'Oh, but it isn't anything to do with business,' she assured the efficient Miss Fane, artlessly, 'it's—well, it's rather personal.'

The other woman said nothing for a moment, but it was clear from her expression that her worst suspicions had been confirmed, and she was more determined than ever to forestall a meeting between her employer and Charlotte if she could. Perhaps she was already a victim of Gerardo's autocratic charm, she gave every sign of it.

'I'm sorry, Miss Grey,' she began, then stopped short and looked across the hall, not quite so confident suddenly.

Charlotte half turned, pretty sure she knew the reason for her sudden change of manner, and as she expected the tall, lean arrogance of Gerardo Cortez came striding from among the gilded arches. He was booted and spurred and he carried a long Spanish quirt in one hand which he tapped absently against one leg as he walked. He seemed to hesitate for a second when he caught sight of Charlotte's golden fairness in the cool shadowy hall, then he changed direction and came swiftly across to them, dismissing María with a careless hand as he came.

'Señorita Grey,' he said, and there was a suggestion of steel in the velvet-soft voice, 'this is an unexpected pleasure.'

Miss Fane, whatever else she lacked, was determined to the point of stubbornness, and she gave Charlotte no time to reply. Her grey eyes fixed on Gerardo's face almost anxiously despite her determination. 'I have told Miss Grey that you are too busy to see anyone this morning, Don Gerardo,' she told him. 'You remember we have a great deal of correspondence to get through.'

Probably the formality of his greeting had given her the idea that Charlotte was claiming a closer relationship than actually existed, for it had scarcely suggested they would have anything of a very personal nature to discuss. It was difficult to judge exactly what his reaction was to her being there, but Charlotte looked at him with a hint of anxiety in her blue eyes.

'I wondered if you'd see me, for just a few minutes,' she pleaded. Her pulse was racing while she bore that black-eyed scrutiny, and her legs felt alarmingly unsteady, but she had to go through with it now—somehow.

'You came alone?'

'Yes.'

He nodded, and she glimpsed a small twist of sardonic amusement at one corner of his mouth. 'I wish only to avoid possible—unpleasantnesses, *señorita*,' he told her, soft-voiced, and it was impossible not to realise that he referred to Luis's hotheaded attempt to hit him.

She cast him a brief reproachful glance and shook her her head. 'I came alone,' she said.

A black brow arched swiftly and amusement glittered for a moment in his eyes. 'And without the knowledge of Luis Berganza, I presume!'

'No one knows I'm here,' she admitted, and he shook his head as if he deplored her rashness in coming. 'I've told you before, Don Gerardo, I don't need anyone's permission—I'm a free agent.'

'Ah! So you did!' Miss Fane was watching them with a look that showed she was both puzzled and irritated, and Charlotte waited, wondering if he really would refuse to talk to her. '*Muy bien!*' He seemed to make up his mind suddenly, and he turned to his secretary with a small and half apologetic smile that for some reason annoyed Charlotte. 'I will be only a few moments, Señorita Fane.'

'Don Gerardo, if you——'

'That is all, *señorita!*' The curt dismissal brooked no argument, but Charlotte sensed the malice that emanated from the other woman as she turned to go. Jealousy was not the prerogative of Luis—Gerardo's secretary suffered from it too.

With a large hand under her arm Charlotte was led across the vast hall and into the room she had been brought to the last time she came, and she could feel the urgent hammering of her heart while his strong fingers were gripping her arm. He opened the door, then stood back to allow her to precede him, and when she passed him in the doorway the warmth of his body brushed against her bare arm. The contact was brief but surprisingly affecting, and she was conscious of a tangy combination of some masculine scent mingled with the unmistakable smell of horses.

'Please, sit down.'

The room was uncannily familiar, although she had spent so little time in it before, and she instinctively chose to sit on the same long, high-backed settee while Gerardo went and stood some distance off with his back to one of the windows. He looked tall and rather dismayingly stern, dressed as he was, much more earthy and vibrantly masculine, with his booted feet set apart in a stance that suggested impatience.

The long boots he wore emphasised the length of his legs, and a fawn shirt, open at the neck, showed a tanned throat, the sleeves rolled back from dark, strong muscular arms. His hands were clasped behind his back, one of them still holding the red-leather quirt, and altogether he presented a vigorous and dominant figure that was stunningly exciting.

Charlotte tried not to watch him, but time and again her eyes were drawn to him, and she still could not put into words what she wanted to say. Indeed, the longer she was with him the harder it became, and she knew he was all too aware of her difficulty, even though with his back to the window she could not see his features very well.

'I—I hope you didn't mind too much, my asking to see you,' she said, and glanced at the door wondering if the cool but jealous Miss Fane was still hovering out there.

Gerardo said nothing for the moment, but shook his head, then he left his place suddenly and came across towards her, standing for a second or two like some disturbing Nemesis, looking down at her with those unfathomable black eyes. It was unexpected and even more disturbing when he sat down beside her, close enough to set her heart pounding heavily when she remembered the last time he had shared the same settee with her.

Then he had taken her in his arms. He had been gentle and comforting, insisting on getting a doctor for her—gentle, that is, until those last few seconds just before Luis came in with María. In those few seconds passion had flared in his black eyes and his mouth on hers had promised the most incredible excitements, excitements that Luis's arrival had defeated.

It was that promise, the warmth of his breath on her mouth and the heart-stopping strength of his arms that made her tremble now when she remembered them, so that she held her palms tightly together in her lap, and brought her mind determinedly back to the reason she was there.

'You find it difficult to say?' Gerardo asked, and Charlotte glanced at him swiftly.

'You—you can guess it's about Luis?'

He nodded, leaning back with one leg drawn up across the other and with the ankle resting on his knee, apparently quite at ease. 'I do not know exactly what you have in mind,' he told her, 'unless it is some form of apology for his behaviour last night. But then I cannot believe that Luis Berganza would delegate someone else to make his apology for him, and certainly not you.' The black eyes fixed themselves with unnerving steadiness on her flushed face for a moment. 'Shall I therefore conclude that you have undertaken to apologise on his behalf without his knowledge?'

An apology was due, Charlotte realised, though it only now occurred to her, and certainly it would be necessary before she could broach the other, much more delicate matter that had brought her there. She hesitated a moment longer, suddenly feeling a sense of panic at the enormity of the task she had set herself, then moistened her lips with the tip of her tongue before she spoke.

'Will—will you accept an apology on Luis's behalf, Don Gerardo?'

He still watched her steadily, and she was finding it increasingly hard to bear. '*Has* he made you his advocate, *pequeña*?' he asked, and the unexpected gentleness in his voice took her by surprise, so that she felt suddenly rather small and breathless. 'Did he send you?'

'Oh no—I mean, I know he'll want to apologise, when he's cooled down a bit, but in the meantime, won't you please take an apology from me?'

A small and infinitely disturbing smile touched the corner of his mouth, and he leaned forward, thudding his booted foot on to the carpet, as he turned to face her. One hand rested on the high back of the settee and he leaned closer to look into her flushed face for a moment before he slid a hand beneath her chin and raised her face.

'Does he mean so much to you that you come here and—humble yourself on his behalf?' His voice was low and vibrant, like the touch of a light finger along her spine, and she shivered. 'Does he, Charlotte?'

'Oh no! I—I mean, not in the same way you're implying.' It was so difficult to think clearly when he sat so close, and his thumb moved with caressing lightness over her jaw. 'I—I just wanted to get things straight before I ask you—something, Gerardo—Don Gerardo.'

She corrected herself hastily, but he was smiling, she noticed in a brief anxious glance at his face. 'I have no objection to your use of my christian name,' he told her, 'though it would not improve relations between Luis Berganza and myself if he were to hear you, I think.' The hand under her chin lifted her face to him suddenly while the intensity of his black gaze fixed itself on her mouth. 'What is it that you wish to ask of me, *mi pequeña*?' he asked softly. 'If it is possible, I will do it.'

In the present circumstances Charlotte found it impossible to think lucidly about anything, so that she eased away from the hand under her chin and sat forward, right to the edge of the seat, and looked down at her hands while she spoke. 'It's rather difficult to know how to put it,' she confessed, and swallowed hard while she sought for the right words. 'You—you must know, as everyone else there did, that the party last night was a—a kind of business gathering, you even spoke about it.'

'*Si*, I know that.'

'Don Agustin knows that Luis lives only a short distance from here, you're neighbours, really, and Luis was supposed to—I mean, Don Agustin expected Luis to talk to you—about business.'

She was putting it very badly, she knew, and she was not doing Luis's cause any good at all by being so irritatingly slow in coming to the point, but she had to go on now, no matter what happened. He was waiting for her to state her case, Luis's case, and she could not suddenly change her mind.

'So?' Gerardo's expression gave nothing away. Thick black lashes hid whatever was in his eyes when he looked along the length of that arrogant nose at her, and only the slightest tightening about his mouth gave her a clue to his reaction—a clue she noted with dismay.

'Please,' she said, breathlessly husky, 'I—I think it might be better if I didn't say any more. I shouldn't have come, I can see that now, but somehow I had to try.' A small, resigned shrug showed that she had given up all hope of his understanding, and her heart was pounding anxiously in case she had made things worse instead of better.

'You wished to discuss business with me?'

'Oh no, of course not!' She shook her head hastily, looking at him from the corner of her eyes. 'Please try and understand—Luis would be furious if he knew I was here, and especially if he knew *why* I was here, but——'

'I would probably be equally furious if I knew why you were here,' Gerardo interrupted coolly,' so perhaps you would be better advised to say no more of the matter, *chica*!'

'But it was partly my fault,' Charlotte insisted anxiously, and he shook his head, laughing shortly.

'Because I kissed you? If such a small and chaste gesture may be termed a kiss! I think not, Charlotte!'

'But if you don't—I mean, if Don Agustin was to learn *why* Luis didn't talk to you as he was supposed to. Oh, how can I put it to make you understand?' She looked at him with wide and anxious eyes, wondering vaguely why he wasn't as furious as he threatened to be. She smoothed down her skirt with restless hands, her face shadowed by the brim of her hat as she lowered her head once more. 'I really shouldn't have come, but I wanted to try and put things right. Instead I'm only making them worse.' Getting to her feet suddenly, she stood for a second on legs that felt alarmingly unsteady. 'I'm sorry, Don Gerardo, I'd better go.'

He too got up and for a second or two they stood facing one another, not quite touching but with such a sense of awareness for each other that the air was as taut as a drum-skin between them, then he reached out and touched her arm. Charlotte started, catching her breath as she looked up at him swiftly.

'I am not a fool, Charlotte,' he said in a voice that could bring chaos to her senses, 'and neither am I vengeful. I know that Don Agustin, among others, hopes to acquire the legal work involved with the business I control, and I know—I can guess, that Luis

131

Berganza was meant to persuade me in his favour. The fact that he behaved like a jealous *novio* does not make the firm that he represents any less capable, and to some degree I find his action understandable.'

Charlotte was staring at him with wide and scarcely believing eyes, her lips parted as she tried to absorb the gist of what he was saying. 'You mean—you mean you won't be influenced by what Luis did last night?'

'Not in the least, business is strictly a matter for practicality!' Laughter glowed in his black eyes and a hint of mockery too, she thought, and he reached out to touch her face with his fingertips. 'Do I disappoint you, *pequeña*?' he asked. 'Had you hoped for a more dramatic battle between your—admirers?'

For a moment Charlotte did not know quite what she felt, and she simply looked at him a little vaguely. She was quite unprepared for him to pull her into his arms, bringing her close to the exciting warmth of him, but she instinctively put up her hands to the broad chest that pulsed with the beat of his heart, and tipped back her head when his mouth came closer. For a second the black eyes blazed down at her and she closed her own slowly until thick lashes brushed her cheeks, barely conscious of a hand that snatched the little white hat from her head before twining strong brown fingers into her silky soft hair.

The promise of his mouth that she remembered so vividly was fulfilled with a breathless excitement that swept her into an experience she had never known before. Her heart beat so fast that she felt it must stop, and her whole body responded to the strong passionate vigour of his, like a willow to the wind. From her mouth to her neck and the vulnerable pulsing softness of her throat, his kisses seemed to draw the very breath from her, and she offered no resistance at all.

'Gerardo!'

She looked up into his face at last and her eyes were huge and jewel-bright as she sought for some sign that he was as moved as she was herself. The black eyes seemed unfathomable, although that deep glowing darkness still showed somewhere in their depths, and his firm mouth showed a hint of smile at its corners. He curved a hand about her cheek and looked down at her, shaking his head slowly.

'I think it is better that you go, *mi pequeña*,' he said in a voice that was barely more than a whisper, then for a moment his mouth was pressed to hers once more. 'Go now, please.'

It seemed incredible that he should be telling her to go and yet there was no doubt that he meant what he said. His voice was soft, even gentle, but edged with that hint of steel, and she drew away from him, though only to the extent of breaking contact with that warm hard body that she found so disturbing. Her hands still rested either side of his neck and she looked up at him, too bewildered for the moment to understand.

'You—you want me to go?'

'It is better that you do, Charlotte.'

'For my own good?' She could not help the bitterness that tinged her words and his black eyes held hers steadily for a second, as if he knew how she was feeling and regretted it without being able to change anything.

'And possibly for mine too,' he said. 'I will not apologise for kissing you, Charlotte, only promise that it will not happen again.'

He sounded so cool and controlled, so final, and heaven knew what she would have said in answer to what was virtually a dismissal, but somewhere behind her, on the other side of that big cool room, she was vaguely aware that a door had opened and of Miss Fane's cool, hard voice apologising for the interruption and informing Gerardo that there was a telephone call for him.

'Señora Fantorini from Madrid,' she told him, and left her opinion in no doubt. 'Shall I ask the caller to ring back, Don Gerardo?'

The dark brassy brunette of last night, Charlotte guessed hazily, and heard Gerardo say, 'No, I will be there in a few moments—ask the *señora* to wait, *por favor.*'

She heard the door close again behind Miss Fane, but kept her eyes on Gerardo's face. He put his big dark hands over hers and held them tightly for a second before lifting them from beside his neck. 'You understand now, *mi pequeña*?' he said, and a tight sardonic smile twisted his mouth for a moment. 'It is better that you go, believe me.'

It took all the nerve she could muster for Charlotte to nod as coolly as she did, when her whole body was shaking with a reaction she did not entirely understand, and she stuck out her chin in a gesture that was unconsciously defiant as she turned to go. She dared not say anything, for she had the horrible feeling that she might cry if she did, and she could not have borne the humiliation of that.

CHAPTER SEVEN

CHARLOTTE had thought it best to say nothing about her impulsive visit to Castillo Cortez and her efforts to put things right for Luis, but for the next couple of days she nursed a curiously angry hurt when she thought about the way she had been sent away. As a man Gerardo Cortez was like no other she had met before and he could arouse emotions in her that were almost frightening in their intensity.

She was not yet ready to admit to being in love with him, only that he could affect her in a way that no one ever had before, and thinking about him brought on a strangely restless feeling that gave her no peace. It was because of the restless feeling that she gladly accepted when Luis asked if she would like to go to a local *feria* with him.

Martha was all in favour of the idea, though she warned her not to expect much similarity between the event they went to and the fairs she was used to at home in England. It promised to be interesting, though, for there would be a *fiesta* and various displays of country skills as well as a horse-jumping competition. Normally she would have questioned anything as traditionally English as show-jumping at a Spanish fair, but at the mention of horses, almost inevitably her thoughts went straight to Gerardo again, and try as she would he was incredibly hard to dismiss.

Despite four months in Spain and the acquisition of a passable tan, she still looked very English in a pale blue dress and sandals, and Martha recognised the fact with an indulgent smile when she saw her together with Luis just before they left the house, a smile that suggested a certain satisfaction at the way things were.

'You make a very handsome pair,' she observed, but Luis pulled a face.

'Not a pair, Mamá, unfortunately,' he told her. 'I only wish we were.'

It was the type of conversation that Charlotte always found a little embarrassing, but no one would ever convince Martha that any woman could go on resisting her handsome son, and she smiled at him confidently. 'Only have patience, darling,' she told him. 'Faint heart never won fair lady, as the saying goes!' Surveying Charlotte in her blue dress but with nothing covering her corn-gold hair, she frowned curiously at her. 'You look lovely, my dear, but shouldn't you be wearing a hat? That little white one you're so fond of would be just right with that pretty dress, why aren't you wearing it today?'

It was a question that Charlotte had been hoping would not have to be answered, although sooner or later either Luis or his mother were bound to mention it. She carefully avoided Martha's eyes and instead swung her long hair back from her face and laughed. 'Oh I think I'm enough of a Spaniard by now, Aunt Martha, to go bareheaded. Besides, it's really time I discarded that hat—I should think everyone must be heartily sick of seeing me wear it by now!'

'Not at all, it's a very pretty hat, and you should wear something on your head if you're going to be standing around outside. Don't you agree, Luis?'

Called upon to take sides, Luis studied Charlotte's silky fair head for a moment or two before passing an opinion. 'Much as I love your beautiful hair, darling,' he said after a second, 'I have to agree with Mamá that

136

you should wear a hat as you usually do. Why *aren't* you wearing it today?'

Charlotte felt rather as if she had been cornered, and her heart beat became suddenly more urgent as she sought for an explanation. It should be easy enough to say that the hat was lost, but it was because she thought she knew where it had been lost that she found it so difficult to explain.

She had been wearing it when she cycled down to the village two days ago, and she had been wearing it immediately before Gerardo kissed her, but after that she was not so clear about anything. Vaguely in the back of her mind was a recollection of it being snatched from her head in the second before strong fingers twined themselves into her hair, from then on all she could clearly remember was the strength and passion of the arms that had held her and the mouth that had deprived her of all sense of time and reason.

'I—I think I must have lost it.' She hastily banished those irresistible but disturbing recollections, but she was not very good at telling an outright untruth, and she laughed nervously as she shook her head. 'Anyway, it's surely time I was acclimatised enough to go bareheaded!'

Whether or not Martha accepted her reason, she frowned over it and it was almost certain she would have said something more on the subject, but Luis, who was content to let her wear anything she pleased as long as she was with him, smiled and put an arm around her shoulders.

'Then go bareheaded, *amante*,' he told her. 'You look lovely as you are, with or without your little hat! Now —shall we go?'

It seemed to Charlotte as if everyone for miles around must have come to San Cristóbal, and the general air of excitement was so infectious that she felt herself touched by it even before they left the car and started to walk. Maybe an outing like this was just what she needed to rid herself of that disturbing restlessness; to banish the disquieting memory of Gerardo's kisses and the feel of his arms around her. Most of all perhaps it would help to make her forget the abrupt way he had sent her packing—for her own good, so he would have had her believe.

Realising that she was yet again dwelling on the very things she sought to forget, she shook herself impatiently and concentrated on what was going on around her. There was a lot going on, although as Martha had predicted, the *feria* did not have much in common with the type of fairs she was used to at home. The very differences, though, added to the interest, and she was determined to enjoy herself now that she was there.

The sight and sound of lottery ticket sellers made an innovation that intrigued her and she could not resist buying a ticket, and she begged Luis to let her spend some time watching a group of dancers and musicians. It was such characters that made the *feria* so distinctively different from the English fair, and she wanted to miss nothing.

She was particularly intrigued by an old water-seller who reminded her of María at Castillo Cortez. She had the same sharp wrinkled features and a complexion that was mahogany dark, with a hawklike nose and jet black eyes. They were faces that Goya might have sketched, and almost beautiful in their own way.

The old water-seller was less neatly and tidily

138

dressed than María, but the similarity was there. A patterned cloth hid most of her grizzled grey hair and she seemed to be wearing several layers of petticoats, despite the intense heat, while walking beside her was a pathetically thin donkey carrying baskets on his back that held fat, potbellied jars of water.

While the patient little beast plodded through the crowd, the woman's harsh, cracked voice could be heard above the babble of sound all around them— '*Agua, agua!*' and they so fascinated Charlotte that she watched them until they disappeared.

It was hot walking among the people who crowded the quite large area set up as the fairground, and Charlotte regretted the loss of her hat quite early on. It took her a while to realise that the fairground was part of the valley immediately below the towering dominance of Gerardo Cortez' castle and when she looked up at it her heart fluttered uneasily, reminded once more of her last visit there.

It was while she was eating some curious sticky sweet concoction in her fingers, some time later, that she looked across to where a temporary car park had been set up, and caught her breath audibly. There could be two cars so much alike, she supposed, but she felt so sure that the one she saw parked there among one or two others, including Luis's, was the one in which Gerardo had so nearly run her down.

Her reaction must have attracted Luis's attention for he looked down at her and smiled inquiringly. Had they been in England and he had been brought up in the less formal atmosphere of his mother's country, Charlotte thought, he would have kissed her—as it was he squeezed her fingers hard, and used his eyes to convey what was in his mind.

'Are you interested in the show-jumping?' he asked. 'It is about to start—shall we watch it?'

Charlotte nodded, glad of the distraction. 'I'd quite like to,' she said. 'I presume it's much as we see at home.'

'Exactly the same,' Luis said, and turned her about so that they walked back the way they had come. 'And if you know anything at all about international show-jumping, then you will know that Spain has produced some excellent riders.'

'Yes, of course, they mostly seem to be army officers, if I remember. Is this an army display?'

He was making a way for them through the crowd, his hand tightly over her arm for fear they became parted, and he shook his head. 'It is open to anyone, and there are some good riders here usually. San Cristóbal is only small, but the Copa de Oro Cortez is the big attraction, of course—it is worth a fortune now.'

The name made her glance up at him swiftly and curiously, and there was nothing she could do about the sudden hard and urgent beat of her heart as she passed her tongue over the dryness of her lips. 'Cortez?' she asked, and Luis nodded, a faintly ironical smile on his face.

'An ancestor of the present incumbent gave a gold cup to be competed for annually, and it's still the cause of some keen competition. Originally it was for simple racing, but for the last couple of decades or so it's been awarded for show-jumping, though it's hardly a sport that gives the local people much chance.' He laughed shortly and for a second the hand holding hers squeezed her fingers almost painfully hard. 'About the only time the locals are ever honoured with his company is when he presents the cup—and I don't doubt he only does it because he can't very well not!'

Charlotte's brain was spinning and her heart was thudding like a drum. For all her good intentions of coming to the *feria* to take her mind off the tormenting memory of Gerardo Cortez, she was not going to be allowed to forget him after all. The reason for his car being there was clear—he was there as the representative of his proud and ancient family. *El amo*—the master, as María called him.

'The lord of the manor!' Luis's bitter words echoed her own thoughts and his voice was flat and harsh. 'He stays just as long as it takes to hand over the cup and make a short speech—autocratic devil!'

Charlotte made no comment. The thought of Gerardo being there was enough to start up the old restlessness again, even though the possibility of their meeting was remote, and she was angry with herself for the way she reacted, even to the mention of him. There was nothing she could do about it, but she sighed inwardly as she followed Luis to the side of the arena.

Standards were well up to those of an English county show, and jumps had been erected around quite a large course, while a tinny relay system was already informing the watchers of the coming events and naming the riders. It was necessary to stand, for there were no seats, and Charlotte silently admitted to herself that she would not have so readily stood for such a length of time in the stifling heat had it not been that she knew Gerardo Cortez was scheduled to appear at some time during the proceedings.

Although she had Luis to lean on for support, by the time the last round had been jumped she was feeling uncomfortably hot and breathless and rather as if she was about to faint. She should have got herself another hat, it was foolish not to have done, for she was used to having her head covered, not exposed to the sun as it had now been for several hours.

All around them people were clapping, and shouting encouraging remarks to the winners as they lined up in the ring to receive their awards, and the crowd seemed to be getting closer and closer, until she felt she was being smothered by those at the back pressing forward for a better view.

She caught the name of Cortez among a welter of rapid Spanish that came over the distorting address system, then the people alongside seemed to sweep back suddenly, and she realised that they were forming a corridor, making a way for a small party of officials. Several portly and solemn-faced men were followed by the tall and unmistakable figure of Gerardo Cortez, and slight ripple of sound rose around her as he strode on towards the ring.

It was her luck to be right at the corner of the crowd where the passageway was formed, and there was no way that he could avoid seeing her. She felt the colour flood swiftly into her face with the sudden violent thudding of her heart, then he turned his head quite deliberately and looked at her directly for a second.

His black eyes gleamed like jet, momentarily serious, but almost immediately glowing with sudden amusement, almost as if he had expected to see her there, she thought. When he drew level with her he inclined his head in the merest hint of a bow, and his voice when he spoke was so low-pitched that it was doubtful if anyone else heard what he said.

'Me alegro de verle, señorita!'

Charlotte caught her breath, scarcely able to believe the whispered message had been meant for her. I am

142

glad to see you—how could he say that to her when he had dismissed her so abruptly when they last met? She felt Luis's hand tighten its grip on her arm, and his reaction made it plain that he had some inkling at least of what had been said, even though he had not heard the words.

He was cursing quietly in Spanish, and his virulence quite startled her. Watching Gerardo walk with his fellow judges into the arena his dark eyes glittered angrily and his fingers were even more cruelly tight around her arm. 'One of these days!' he threatened under his breath.

Charlotte's eyes had a curiously dazed look. The tall figure in the arena fascinated her and she found it impossible to take her eyes off him, even when her head began to swim and the voice over the relay system became distant and oddly blurred. She thought he looked at her, and for a second only the black eyes held hers, narrowed below drawn brows.

The hours she had spent standing in the sun and hemmed in by the pressing heat of the crowd began to tell, and she could feel herself begin to slowly sway while her head pounded like a drum in time with the sickeningly heavy thud of her heart. Reaching out instinctively for something to cling to, she clutched anxiously at Luis, and tried desperately not to faint.

'Please, Luis—get me out of here,' she whispered huskily, and his arm slid round her as he glanced behind them for a way through.

There was no hope of making passage through the crowd that pressed ever closer as the prize-giving began, and they seemed to be trapped where they were. It was something to be thankful for that they were at least on the edge of the crowd and not in the middle of it somewhere, so that when Charlotte lost consciousness at last, Luis was able to let her down gently on to the grass.

The murmur of voices around her seemed to alternately increase in volume and die away as she clung anxiously to consciousness for as long as she could, with Luis's voice saying her name urgently and repeatedly. Then suddenly there was nothing at all.

She was quite unaware, as Luis was, that as she slid to the ground Gerardo Cortez took one swift, impulsive step in their direction, his tall figure stiffly urgent suddenly—then just as swiftly he seemed to recover himself, even before his fellow judges could realise there was anything happening.

The crowd pressed further forward and the tinnyvoiced announcements went on. Only very briefly was the mood of the exciting moment changed, and the centre of interest switched from the arena while Luis carried her away in his arms.

It was in the cool shade of a green canvas tent that Charlotte came to, and she found herself looking into the serenely smiling face of a young nun. 'You are feeling recovered, *señorita*?' Her voice was soothingly light and she spoke in clear pedantic English, so that Charlotte smiled reassuringly as she sat up on the edge of a canvas cot bed.

'Oh yes, thank you, I'm fine now.' She indicated her uncovered head and pulled a face. 'I should have worn a hat— I *was* warned.'

'It is always wiser to cover the head,' her attendant agreed smilingly. She put a cool hand to her brow and shook her head when Charlotte started to get up. 'You should not be in too much haste, *señorita*.'

They both looked across swiftly when someone appeared for a moment in the doorway, before hastily ducking back out of sight, except as a shadow on the canvas wall. Her heavy shoes whispering over the grass and her benign smile still in place, the young Sister walked over to see him, and the shadow once more became a man. A curiously uneasy man who acted as if he thought the green canvas tent as sacred as the confines of a convent.

He handed over a small packet and said something that was too quiet for Charlotte to hear, but which obviously puzzled the Sister, for she frowned over it and asked a question. The man shrugged, making it evident, even from a distance, that he was merely a messenger and probably an unwilling one. Then he too seemed to be asking a question and both heads were turned briefly in Charlotte's direction. She watched curiously while the Sister spoke rapidly for a few seconds, then waited until the man disappeared once more, before coming back to her.

She offered the packet to Charlotte. 'For you, señorita. The man said that you would know from whom it came.'

A curious reaction was stirring in Charlotte as she held the soft, tissue-wrapped package in her hands for a second or two, and she tried to make sense of the fact that Gerardo Cortez' name kept coming to mind. It was the Sister's gently curious gaze that prompted her at last to undo the enfolding tissue, and she recognised the contents almost at once.

There was no mistaking the lacy brim of the little white hat she had so recently claimed was lost, and she caught her breath as she took it from the tissue with trembling hands. It was only when she opened it out that she found a note with it—a page hastily torn from a pocket notebook and written in big, bold script, in obvious haste.

'You forgot your hat, *pequeña*, and it seems you have no other!'

It was not signed, but it had no need of a signature. It was impossible that there had been time since she fainted for him to have sent for the hat, so it was obvious he had had it with him with the intention of returning it, and she recalled how his first sight of her out there in the crowd had seemed to suggest that he expected to see her. It was logical, when she considered, for the *feria* was an important local event, and he could be pretty sure that Luis would bring her.

She was aware suddenly that she was being watched, although the Sister's eyes were hastily averted when she looked at her, and she supposed she should offer some kind of explanation. 'I—I thought I'd lost my hat for good,' she said, and laughed a little unsteadily. 'It's lucky someone found it, since it's the only hat I possess!'

'You do not know that it was returned to you by Don Gerardo Cortez?' The light voice sounded doubtful, but a faint smile touched her mouth for a second when Charlotte looked surprised at her knowledge. 'Señor Mendoza delivered the package on behalf of his employer,' the Sister explained. 'He did not mention a name, but I know that the father of the two little Mendoza girls who attend the convent school is employed as Don Gerardo's *criado*.'

'Oh, I see.'

It would do no good to hope that the gesture of returning her hat would simply be put down to it having been found a moment ago, for it would hardly have been returned as carefully wrapped in tissue if that

146

were the case, nor accompanied by a note.

'Don Gerardo also expressed the hope that you are quite recovered,' the light voice went on, 'and I took the liberty of informing him that you had merely fainted in the heat and you were now feeling quite better.' There was only polite inquiry in her eyes when she looked at Charlotte. 'I hope that I did the correct thing, *señorita?*'

'Oh yes—yes, you did, thank you, Sister.'

It was difficult to try and guess whether or not her companion had seen any significance in the gesture of her hat being returned in the way it was. Maybe Gerardo's reputation was as well known to those living in the cloistered confines of the convent as to the village people, but whether it was or not, she was suddenly anxious to be gone before anything more was said.

There was something discomforting about sitting there in the company of this serene-faced and slightly unworldly woman, when every time her fingers encountered the lacy brim of the hat she held on her lap, she was reminded of how Gerardo had snatched it from her head a second before her senses were stunned by the fierce and passionate excitement of his kisses.

'I—I ought to go,' she ventured, 'or Señor Berganza might begin to think I'm really ill.'

'You do not wish to take a few moments longer?'

Her discomfiture had not gone unnoticed, Charlotte realised ruefully, and she began to wonder if the young nun was quite as unworldly as she had supposed. She got to her feet and was relieved to find herself quite steady again, although she still felt curiously on edge.

'Oh no, I'll be all right now, Sister, thank you—I'm grateful for your help.'

She made a more practical gesture of thanks by way of an offertory box on her way out, but anxious eyes still noted her uncovered head. 'Will you not wear your hat now that it has been returned to you, *señorita*?' Charlotte glanced at the tightly rolled bundle in her hand and hesitated. 'It would be wiser,' the quiet insistent voice went on.

It would also mean explaining its reappearance to Luis. Charlotte thought, and felt momentarily at a loss. She rolled the soft package even more tightly and smiled as she walked ahead to the entrance. 'I'm not always as wise as I should be,' she confessed, but made no attempt to explain her meaning.

She had scarcely stepped through the opening into the sun again when Luis was beside her and he took her hand in his, looking down at her for a moment anxiously. 'Charlotte—are you all right?'

Nodding, she glanced over her shoulder rather anxiously at the figure in the dark habit, hovering just behind her. 'I'm fine now, Luis.' She smiled up at him reassuringly. 'It was only a faint.'

'Too much sun and no hat.' Luis declared unhesitatingly.

'I suppose so.'

She turned to say a last word of thanks and her voice was too bright, she realised, too determinedly cheerful. The nun was curious, it showed in her eyes no matter how quickly she sought to conceal it, and Charlotte wanted to be away before she once more urged her to wear her hat.

'*Señorita*, your——' she began, but Charlotte interrupted, her words short and a little breathless, overriding whatever it was she had been going to say.

'Thank you again, Sister, I'll be fine now!'

For a second only, their eyes met and Charlotte saw the dawn of understanding; the recognition of the cause for her anxiety. Then the other's head was bowed and the wimple cast an all concealing shadow across her face. 'Take care, *señorita*,' she said as she turned to go, and Charlotte was left in no doubt that it was not only exposure to the heat of the sun that she had been warned against.

'You *must* take care, darling.' Luis's voice spoke quite close to her ear, and she brought herself hastily back to reality, her heart thudding hard in her breast. His fingers squeezed her lightly and he drew her along beside him. 'I shall take you home,' he said.

'Oh, must we?' She was not even sure why she wanted to stay, only that she felt rather as if she was waiting for something to happen, and it was an uneasy feeling that put brittleness in to her voice. 'Surely there are other things to see, aren't there?'

'I think you should rest for a while, *amante*, you are not as well as you would have me believe and I do not like the idea of you walking about in the sun and possibly becoming really ill with sunstroke. There will be fireworks later, but we can see those from the house.'

'But, Luis——'

'I insist!' Taking her silence for acquiescence, he looked down at her and smiled, his dark eyes warm and glowing as he shook his head slowly. 'I am concerned for you, *amante*,' he told her in a voice that was several octaves lower than usual, 'but also I have an irresistible desire to kiss you, my Charlotte, and I cannot do so here, among all these people!'

She should not have been surprised, and yet somehow she was, and she looked up at him with wide and slightly puzzled eyes. What troubled her most was realising that she did not want Luis to kiss her. When he had done so in the past, she had accepted it without feeling anything but a pleasant sense of satisfaction. Now, suddenly, she did not want him to kiss her at all, and it added to her confusion when the recollection of a fierce hard mouth and strong arms came back to her so vividly that she could almost feel them.

'I will leave you here for a moment while I fetch the car so that you need not walk far.' Luis's voice broke in to her reverie, and she nodded a little vaguely.

'Yes. Yes, I'll wait here in the shade.'

'A moment only!'

He squeezed her fingers and smiled, then left her beside a small temporary hut that had been put up to display baskets, and whose shadow sheltered her from the sun. She watched him stride off in the direction of the car park, then gave her attention to the passing crowd, her gaze idly flitting from one place to another until she picked out a familiar face suddenly, and stared. Her heart leapt in sudden recognition as Gerardo's tall, authoritative figure made his way towards her—or more probably towards the car park.

He saw her in almost the same instant, and for a moment she thought his step slowed, almost stopped, before he came on. He was unmistakable in any crowd, and she wished she could do something about the sudden shakiness of her limbs and the warm flush in her cheeks that had not been there only seconds before. The hasty glance she gave over her shoulder was instinctive rather than voluntary, and Gerardo obviously noticed it, for a ghost of a smile tugged for a moment at his mouth as he came nearer.

A light fawn suit and cream shirt were smooth civilised garb for the arrogantly suggestive savagery of that lean body, and his face looked boldly dark in the harsh brassy light of the sun, his black eyes glowing like jet between their short thick lashes. He came to her without hesitation, as if Luis's possible proximity did not concern him, and he inclined his head briefly before he spoke.

'*Buenas tardes, señorita.*' Just as if he had not murmured that provocative message as he passed her at the edge of the arena earlier, or sent that boldly scrawled note with her hat, Charlotte thought dazedly. His black eyes swept swiftly and searchingly over her face. 'Are you feeling better?'

'Much better, thank you.'

The smile showed in his eyes too, a glimpse of warmth that caused a curling thrill of reaction and set her heart pounding harder than ever. 'How could I know that the little white hat was the only one you possessed?' he asked, in a voice that was like velvet, and shivered through her whole body. 'You were foolish to stand so long in the sun without one, *pequeña*—if I had realised, I would have sent Mendoza with it before.' Laughter threaded his voice and he held her wavering glance determinedly. 'I was only afraid that it might prove embarrassing for you, *chica*!'

Charlotte evaded the steady gaze hastily, and looked at the small crumpled bundle in her right hand. 'It could still,' she confessed. 'Luis doesn't know I have it back yet.'

He was looking beyond her, she noticed suddenly, and the more sharp, narrow look about his eyes told her that Luis was on his way back with the car. She turned, almost reluctantly she realised, as Luis got out, the clumsiness of his movements betraying the depth of his anger when he saw her with Gerardo. His eyes

151

gleamed with it as he came to join them, his fingers fastening tightly around Charlotte's arm.

'Señor!' Gerardo's quiet voice acknowledged his arrival with no visible emotion, then he gave his attention once more to Charlotte, though there was nothing now in either his manner or his expression to which Luis could take exception. He was simply a neighbour who had been politely inquiring after her health. 'I am relieved to know that you are quite recovered, Señorita Grey. Will you now excuse me? I have another appointment shortly.'

She nodded, a small and rather jerky nod, for she could well imagine the kind of appointment he was hurrying off to keep, and her own almost violent dislike of the idea both surprised and disturbed her. 'Yes, of course, Don Gerardo—thank you for your concern.'

He made a barely perceptible bow to each of them in turn and the hint of a polite smile on the straight mouth gave no possible cause for offence. Such cool formality when she remembered the way he had kissed her such a short time ago, and the crushing force of his arms holding her close seemed hardly credible to Charlotte and she had an almost irresistible urge to do almost anything to rouse him from his cool, polite control.

'Señor—Señorita, adiós!'

Goodbye, Charlotte thought wildly, not even until we meet again; and she felt her legs become oddly unsteady as she watched him walk off in the direction of the car park. She brought herself hastily back to earth only when Luis's hand on her arm drew her across to his car. While Luis was walking round to take his place behind the wheel, she took a last quick look back over her shoulder, but not once did the black eyes turn in her direction and she felt a sudden and sickening sense of defeat that she could not quite understand.

Inevitably, the simple fact that she had fainted from standing too long in the sun became a dramatic collapse in Luis's telling, and not for the first time Charlotte regretted his penchant for overstatement. Martha was eyeing her anxiously and even when she tried to deny it had ever been as serious as he made it sound, she could see that Martha was still doubtful.

Luis was not in the best of humours, but his mother put it down to worry about Charlotte's health, and she wanted to make quite sure it was not as bad as he said. 'I do hope you're not suffering from sunstroke, my dear,' she said. 'I think perhaps it might be advisable to call in Doctor Lopez, just to make sure. After that other unfortunate business, when you had a bang on the head, we can't be too careful.'

'Aunt Martha, I'm all right, honestly!' Charlotte looked up at Luis standing beside her chair, and pulled a face at him. 'You know how Luis exaggerates.'

'I was concerned about you,' Luis insisted. His good-looking face took on a hard look and his mouth tightened, so that she could guess what was in his mind. 'I was, and still am, as concerned as Cortez.' He caught his mother's swift, puzzled look and laughed shortly, watching Charlotte as he did so, as if he expected some kind of reaction. 'El amo was lying in wait,' he said, bestowing the title with heavy sarcasm. 'As soon as I went to fetch the car, he moved in to ask how she was.'

'What else did you expect him to do in the circumstances—ignore me?' Charlotte's voice shook with anger at the way he worded his accusation. 'He was on his way to fetch his car, as you were, Luis, and he saw me standing there. He must have seen me make an idiot of myself by fainting, standing where we were he was bound to, and you know perfectly well that he wouldn't just walk past me without asking how I was, any more than you would have done! Anyway,' she added, as if that fact at least was unarguable, 'you were only gone a few minutes!'

'Charlotte——'

'You're being unreasonable, and you know it!'

He hated it when she defended herself against his accusations and usually made the first attempt to heal the breach. He ran a hand through the thick dark hair over his brow and sighed. 'I suppose I am worried about you still,' he said by way of justification, and Charlotte shook her head.

'I just stood too long in the sun and I fainted, that's all.'

'You really shouldn't have gone without a hat, dear,' Martha interposed hastily. 'If you've lost your own you could have borrowed one of mine for today.'

Mention of her hat was the last thing Charlotte wanted at the moment for she had no idea as yet how she was going to explain its return. Ever since they left the *feria* she had had it tightly rolled in her hand, and the wonder was that Luis had not noticed it—if he had been less preoccupied with disliking Gerardo Cortez he might have done so. It was instinctive, but unfortunate, that she chose that moment to glance down at it, for Martha followed her glance and smiled, nothing loath to change the subject.

'You've been shopping,' she guessed. 'Have you bought yourself a new hat, my dear? Do let me see!'

She was smiling and quite unaware that there was

154

anything awkward or difficult about her request, but for the first time Luis took note of the small package in Charlotte's hand and frowned over it curiously.

'You didn't do any shopping,' he said, and ignored his mother's attempt to object to his tone. 'I carried you into the first aid tent and you weren't carrying anything then. I met you when you came out again and you didn't go anywhere after that except to——' He narrowed his eyes and came round to stand directly in front of her. 'You were talking to Cortez—did he give you something?'

'Luis, darling!' Martha made her objection heard at last, but Luis was not ready to let it drop or admit that he had no right to be curious, even accusing.

'I'm just curious,' he insisted. 'What is it that you're holding on to so tightly, darling?'

Charlotte felt trapped. If only she could have chosen her own time, her own way of telling him that she had her hat back, but he had forced the issue and now she had to think quickly. 'Gerardo gave me nothing,' she insisted in a small but clear voice that shook despite her efforts to steady it. 'A—a man brought my hat, wrapped as it is now, to the tent when I was still with the Sister, and if you don't believe that, ask her—she's unlikely to lie to you!'

'Your hat?' He looked stunned for a moment, but it was obvious that he took her word for what had happened. 'Someone found your hat and brought it——' He laughed suddenly, a wild, uninhibited laugh of sheer relief. 'Oh, darling, why did you not tell me so?' He bent to kiss her mouth, a hard, fervent kiss that was quite unlike the way he usually kissed her, and he put a hard strong arm around her shoulders, pulling her close.

155

'Oh, *amante, mi bella, mi amor*—you tease me, *verdad*?' He always became so much more Spanish when he was emotional, and his English became lost in a welter of Spanish endearments as he hugged her. 'So—someone found your little white hat and you are so well known for your hat that it was returned to you!'

He was still laughing when he took the package from her, and she had no time to stop him before he opened it up and shook the hat free of its enfolding tissue. 'You are so well known in San Cristóbal, *mi amor*, that——' He stopped speaking suddenly and his eyes followed the scrap of white paper that fluttered to the floor when he opened up the crown of the hat to balance it on one finger.

Charlotte's head was pounding like a steam hammer, and she sat quite still on her chair while Luis bent to retrieve Gerardo's note—it was useless to try and stop him now, or to say anything, for no one was going to believe anything she said, truth or not. She thought about Gerardo and how she had succumbed so easily and so willingly to his kisses, while all the time he had been ready to discard her as soon as the telephone rang and some woman at the other end demanded his attention.

She had risked losing Luis's trust and Martha's respect to keep the secret of her visit to Castillo Cortez, and now it was all coming out. That brief note spoke for itself—it explained without words where she had been and with whom, and Luis would put his own interpretation on its brief message. He handed it to his mother in silence, then turned and looked at Charlotte as if he could not believe any of it.

'*Madre de Dios*,' he whispered harshly, 'I will kill him!'

CHAPTER EIGHT

IT would be silly of her not to expect things to be different from now on, Charlotte knew, but she was not prepared for the very different atmosphere that seemed to divide their small company in to two entirely opposite sides. Martha was as much hurt as angry, but Charlotte could understand her reaction to some extent, for not only had she turned down the idea of marrying Luis, but she had paid a secret and highly controversial visit to the home of Gerardo Cortez.

She had no excuse, for she was fully conversant with Spanish proprieties by now, and she was perfectly well aware of how Luis felt about Gerardo. No matter what her reason had been for going to the castle, and whether or not her motive had been to help Luis, the fact of her going at all was simply not acceptable.

'I don't know what else I can say,' Charlotte told them huskily, and flicked the tip of her tongue hastily over her dry lips. 'I—I wanted to help Luis, and seeing Gerardo—Don Gerardo seemed the best way to do it. I thought that if I could explain to him——'

'Explain?' Martha's usually friendly eyes held none of their more familiar warmth and encouragement. 'My dear child, what could you possibly say to Don Gerardo that could help Luis?'

If only Charlotte could have been sure which of them she should appeal to, it would have helped—she felt rather as if she was facing a court of inquiry, although so far Luis had said very little. He sat in his chair with his hands clasped tightly together in front of him, and his eyes looked smoulderingly dark and angry as he watched her.

Martha had her customary needlework with her, but it lay neglected on her lap so far; instead she was looking directly at Charlotte, except for the occasional glances she gave her son, glances that seemed almost apologetic to Charlotte. As if she felt a certain sense of responsibility for his present anger and unhappiness because it had been she who brought Charlotte into their home.

'What did you hope to achieve by doing anything as rashly foolish as going to the castle?' Martha was set on getting to the bottom of it, and since it was a matter that concerned her adored son, she was unlikely to spare anyone in the process. 'Surely you know by now how Luis feels about Gerardo Cortez? I would have thought that was reason enough for you to stay well away from the man!'

'I went with the best of intentions, Aunt—Mrs Berganza.' She stumbled over the formality; for the privilege of calling her employer by a more intimate title seemed out of place at the moment, and she felt suddenly as if she had never been so alone in her life before. Her voice was horribly unsteady and she darted a swift, reproachful look at Luis when he snorted his disbelief in her good intentions. 'I just thought that if I could make him realise that Don Agustin's firm was in no way——'

'*Madre mia!*' Luis swore softly, staring at her in disbelief. 'You actually went there to discuss the business affairs of Don Agustin with him?'

'Oh no, of course I didn't—how could I?' She was very close to tears and at the moment she wanted nothing so much as to go somewhere alone. Only if she left now, with the matter still in the air, it would suggest something to hide, that she admitted some kind of guilt, and she refused to admit that. Instead she tried once more to explain her impulsive visit to the castle. 'I simply wanted to explain that because you—reacted the way you did to——'

'Seeing you making love with him in the garden!' Luis interposed with heavy irony, and Charlotte shook her head firmly.

'It was nothing like that, Luis, and you know it!'

'If you felt no guilt about what happened, then I do not see why you had the need to put matters right,' he insisted. 'If that *was* why you went to see him!'

Charlotte's eyes had a bright, shimmering look that threatened tears, and her voice was shakily unsteady no matter how she tried to control it. 'You have only my word for it, Luis! I thought that if I told Don Gerardo why you were there, and that you acted on impulse, that you were likely to be in trouble with——'

'You went to plead? For *me*?' His dark eyes blazed at her and only then did she see the full implication of what she had done. She could almost feel the hurt to his pride herself as he glared across at her, and when he got to his feet suddenly, she caught her breath. '*Madre de Dios!*' he breathed piously. 'You dare to beg the understanding of this man—for *my* sake!'

'I wanted to help, Luis.' She picked on the one bright spot in the whole mess and looked across at him hopefully. 'I have his word that he means to employ Don Agustin's firm anyway.'

Luis's lip curled. 'I will not ask how you achieved this—act of persuasion, I think I would dislike that answer even more than those I have heard so far!'

'Luis!'

She would have liked to be able to swear that she had gone to see Gerardo purely and simply for the purpose of helping to put matters right for him, but now, for the first time, she knew she hadn't. The idea of being once more in Gerardo's arms and of rekindling the scene that Luis's arrival had interrupted the first time, had been in the back of her mind all the time. The realisation stunned her for a moment and she could not think clearly.

'You ask me to accept that you had nothing to do with his decision, Charlotte, when you admit you went there to persuade him?'

The hard bright look in his eyes was infinitely discomfiting. It seemed to see too deeply into her private thoughts and she glanced swiftly at Martha before getting to her feet. She stood for a moment trying to find the right words, trying to believe that she was actually about to bring this wonderful life to an end.

Her brain spun and her thoughts were a chaotic jumble as she faced the fact of nothing being the same any more. The familiar, cosy atmosphere she was used to was no longer a fact, and she was unprepared for losing it so abruptly. Her legs were shakily unsteady and her hands trembled as she held them tightly together, but she saw no other solution, and pressed on.

'I—I don't quite know how to go about this,' she said, addressing herself to Martha because she looked slightly less severe than Luis did. 'It's rather sudden and I've never really prepared myself for giving you notice, but——'

'Charlotte!'

'Now I imagine it's the best thing to do—the only thing for me to do.' She laughed, but it was laughter devoid of any hint of humour and sounded shakily unsteady, and she hurried on when it looked as if Martha was about to say something. 'I—I can either

160

work out a month's notice, or go right away. I imagine the sooner I'm gone the better in the circumstances.' She looked directly at Martha Berganza's slightly dazed expression, then lost sight of her face altogether suddenly when the tears flooded into her eyes. 'I'm—I'm sorry about this, Aunt Martha, I'm sorry it had to end like this, but——'

'Oh, Charlotte, my dear child, it doesn't have to end like this at all! I cannot imagine why you want to take such a drastic action, when——'

'I can't stay where I'm no longer trusted, Aunt Martha!' It was hard to speak when she felt so choked, and she turned away, heading for the door but never really sure how she got there. It was ridiculous to think that she could simply walk out and never come back, but at the moment it was what she wanted to do, and she hurried across the hall only vaguely aware of the heavy silence she left in the big room. A silence suddenly broken by Luis's voice calling out her name.

'Charlotte! Charlotte!'

He was coming after her, she could tell, and it lent speed to her flight. She was more than half way up the stairs by the time he came out into the hall, and she did not even pause when he started to follow her. Where she would go to avoid him, she had no idea, for she could only stay in her room for so long; sooner or later she would have to come out, and sooner or later she would have to face Luis again.

'Charlotte, wait!'

Her bedroom door cut off the rest of what he said, and she leaned her back against it for a few seconds almost as if she expected him to follow her in there. His feet on the carpet outside the door had a firm determined tread and they came to a halt abruptly, a second before he began to tap on the door with his knuckles.

'Charlotte, please, listen to me!'

'It's no use, Luis!' She was crying in earnest, and her voice sounded husky and choked. 'There's nothing to talk about.'

He waited a second, then rapped again. 'Just for a few seconds, please, Charlotte.'

She put her hands to her mouth, trying to stifle the sobs that gave her voice a curiously abrupt and breathless sound, shaking her head even though he could not see her. 'It's—no good—Luis, I—I'm going, there's nothing else I can do.'

'You could talk to me!'

His voice had a trace of the familiar coaxing tone she had heard so often, and for a moment she glanced over her shoulder at the solid darkness of the door between them, then she shook her head. 'What good would it do?' she asked!'

'Please, Charlotte!'

It would be so easy to be persuaded, she thought, and shook her head determinedly, her hands rolled tightly at her sides. 'I don't feel like talking, Luis, not yet.' She swallowed hard, and wondered if she ever would feel like discussing Gerardo with him—he was suddenly much more of a stranger to her than he had ever been. 'Leave me alone for a while,' she pleaded. 'I need to think, Luis, please.'

He said nothing for a moment, but she could imagine the slight shrug of his shoulders when he yielded at last, and his voice sounded touchingly reluctant when he agreed. 'As long as you talk to me about it before you do anything—silly, *amante*, eh?'

She did not answer and, after a moment or two, she heard him move off, and guessed he had gone back downstairs to rejoin his mother. It must have come as a shock to Martha, her deciding to leave like that, but she really felt it would be for the best in the long run. She wasn't in love with Luis, and she was far too close to being in love with Gerardo Cortez—in such a situation it was impossible for the old relationship with Luis and his mother to continue.

With Gerardo coming yet again to mind, she sighed as she brushed the tears from her face and walked across to the window in sudden restlessness, looking across to where the glowering bulk of Castillo Cortez cast its shadow over the valley immediately below it. It was becoming more and more certain that she was falling in love with the arrogant and sophisticated man who lived there and the only possible solution to that situation was to go home to England and forget about him—anything else was quite out of the question.

With another deep sigh, she turned and picked up the little white hat that lay on the bed, looking at it for a second before pulling it on over her corn-gold hair. It had caused her present trouble and she almost hated the sight of it, but it was the only hat she possessed and if she was going out she needed to wear one. Going out was perhaps a possible cure for her present restlessness—let her mind go blank for a while and she would probably see things more clearly.

No one had seen her leave, and Charlotte had no qualms about not saying anything to anyone. From the very beginning Martha had worked towards one end, that of seeing her son married to her old friend's daughter, and Charlotte felt she needed to think for herself for a change. Martha had been kind to her, but between them she and Luis had done a great deal to try and pressure her into something she did not want, and she wanted to make up her own mind.

Heaven knew why she had chosen to walk when she could have taken her bicycle, but in the first place she had not intended coming so far. She was almost into the village and the sun was as hot as it always was at this time of day, much too hot to encourage her to turn around and walk back, uphill all the way.

She was about to take the last bend into the village square when a car came round the corner, going in the opposite direction, and she skipped hastily back out of harm's way. It was big and black and easily recognisable as the one belonging to Gerardo Cortez, and for a second her heart thudded so hard in her breast that she felt sure it must stop.

'Charlotte!' It was remarkable that he could pull up in so short a distance, and he was turned in his seat looking back at her over his shoulder, his black eyes bright and curious.

She could not resist turning round too, and she looked at him for a moment almost in despair. Her mind was in chaos as she tried to tell herself that Gerardo Cortez was the very last person she wanted to see in her present mood, and yet her heart persisted in hammering hard and fast as she looked at him, as if even seeing him there on the road excited her.

She walked back towards him scarcely knowing she was doing it, and he was out of his seat in a moment, standing there waiting for her, with his black eyes watching her every step of the way, deep and unfathomable. A light fawn suit looked businesslike despite the fact that he wore no tie with the blue shirt, and she wondered what had possessed him to stop and speak to her.

He said nothing for a moment when she joined him, but after a second or two a hand slid beneath her chin and raised her face, the hard palm warm and smooth on her soft skin, his thumb caressingly gentle on her jaw as he studied her face in silence.

'You have been crying,' he said, and shook his head when she would have denied it. 'What is wrong, *pequeña*?'

'How did you—how did you know I'd been crying?' She asked the question only because she did not want to tell him that he had been the reason for her tears. 'Is that why you stopped?'

He was smiling and somehow she found it very reassuring, though she was not quite sure why. 'I have good sight,' he told her, 'but even I cannot detect tears while travelling in a car at the speed I was going, Charlotte!' He used one long finger to brush her thick wet eyelashes, and his laughter was soft and deep, barely audible even on the still hot air. 'I do not know why I stopped, since you ask me,' he confessed. 'But now that I have, will you not tell me why you have been crying, *pequeña*?'

'It—it was nothing really.' She could not tell him that his note, those few hastily scribbled words, had caused a scene that was likely to alter her whole way of life. 'I—Luis and I had a difference of opinion.'

'You quarrelled?'

She supposed that brief and bitter exchange had been a quarrel, and she nodded. It should not matter to him one way or the other, but at the moment that did not occur to her—it was good enough that he was someone she could talk to who was not likely to be biased against her.

'I suppose we did,' she admitted, and her eyes were

downcast as she tried to still the frantic urgency of her heartbeat. His being close was no less disturbing than it always was, and she found herself wishing she could be in the strong comforting closeness of his arms again. 'I've decided to leave and—and go home.'

She did not quite know what to make of his silence, but it would be too optimistic to expect he would express regret at the idea of her going away—even so she nursed a small hope in her heart that he might. It was a second or two before he reached out and touched her cheek lightly with a finger-tip.

'You are feeling very small and very unhappy, eh, *pequeña*?' he asked, soft-voiced, and she nodded without speaking. 'Then perhaps it would bring some comfort if I offered to take you to lunch, huh?'

Charlotte looked up at him swiftly, her blue eyes wide and blank for a moment. It was difficult to take the invitation seriously in view of their past encounters, and yet he was hardly likely to joke about it, and she blinked herself hastily back to earth when she realised he was still waiting for an answer. 'Weren't you—aren't you on your way—somewhere?' she asked, and he smiled slowly.

'I hope I am on my way to lunch with you, *pequeña* —what do you say? Will you come?' He looked down at her simple pale green cotton dress as if he anticipated her using its unsuitability as an excuse not to accept. 'You look very sweet and very proper in that dress too, so there is no need for you to refuse on *its* account!'

It took Charlotte only a moment to make up her mind. No one knew she had left the house, so if she did not appear for lunch as likely as not it would be assumed that she was still in her room. The idea of lunching with Gerardo was irresistible, whatever the

166

circumstances, and she sounded curiously breathless as she accepted.

'I'd love to have lunch with you, Don Gerardo—thank you.'

Laugher gleamed in his eyes as he took her arm and saw her in to the car. 'Am I still to be called Don Gerardo even though we are lunching together?' he asked.

Colour flooded her face and caused her even more embarrassment, but she kept her eyes averted while he closed the door on her and walked around to his own seat. A swift sideways glance at those strong, arrogant features set her heart hammering furiously, and there was a curious curling sensation in her stomach when he slid into the seat beside her, his sleeve brushing her bare arm.

He started the engine, then sat for a moment with his hands on the wheel, looking down at her over his shoulder and with one black brow arched in query, so that once more she avoided his gaze. 'Perhaps it is as well,' he murmured, without explaining his reasoning, and with a shake of his head he set the big car moving.

Charlotte sat back, feeling curiously pleased with the way things had turned out, and not in the least troubled about driving off to have lunch with him with no one the wiser as yet. Whatever happened when she got back was unimportant at the moment, and all she could think about was being with Gerardo—that fact filled her with an incredible sense of satisfaction.

Such delicious lobster, and in such quantity, could only be followed by fresh fruit for dessert, and Charlotte had seldom enjoyed a meal more. A delicate Rioja wine had given her a slightly light-headed feeling, but nothing more. Only enough to put a faint flush of colour into her cheeks and a soft glowing look in her eyes as she savoured the last mouthful of fresh fig.

Not another word had been said about the quarrel with Luis, and that was how she preferred it to be, but if there was one trait that Luis and Gerardo had in common it was a determination never to let a matter drop once it had been raised. She had scarcely time to swallow her last mouthful of fig before Gerardo was looking at her with a raised brow.

'I cannot help suspecting that I was in some way responsible for your quarrel with Luis Berganza,' he said. 'Was Mendoza, my groom, less discreet than he might have been when he returned your hat, perhaps? He brought it at the wrong moment?'

'Oh no, not at all!' Charlotte looked down hastily at her empty plate, unwilling to discuss it, but unable to see a way of avoiding it at the moment. 'In fact he gave it to the nun in charge of the first-aid tent—Luis knew nothing about it until we got home.'

His black eyes sought and held hers for a moment. 'He knew nothing of it when I spoke to you at the *feria*?'

'Nothing—not then.'

'And yet he was angry, even then.' He mused on the fact as if it intrigued him to speculate, then he smiled briefly and shook his head. 'He is a very jealous man, *pequeña*, he must love you very much.'

Charlotte frowned, shaking her head in case he should imagine it pleased her to have such a handsome and jealous lover. '*Too* jealous,' she told him, leaving her own feelings in no doubt, 'and with no cause.' She caught his eye and hurried on. 'He doesn't have the right to be jealous, and I find it an increasing embarrassment. He—he claims to love me, but he knows that I don't feel the same way about him, and whatever the situation was, he has no *cause* to be jealous.'

'No?' He questioned her certainty, then went on before she could reply. 'Is he aware of your last visit to *el castillo*, Charlotte?'

'Yes.' She looked up, not blaming him, but simply trying to explain. 'When he saw your note inside my hat, he—he knew.'

'I am sorry, *pequeña.*'

An apology from him was the last thing she expected or wanted, and she shook her head hastily. 'Oh, but it didn't really matter!'

It mattered a great deal, she thought, for it had changed her whole life. In fact he had been doing that each time they met ever since that first eventful episode. He leaned closer suddenly and his voice had a deep quietness that was almost a physical touch that shivered over her skin, like steel in velvet.

'I do not think I can believe that,' he told her, and she looked down at her hands rather than across at him.

'It was something that was bound to happen sooner or later,' she insisted in a small unsteady voice. 'Luis behaves as if he has every right to be jealous, and he makes it impossible for me to live my own life without accounting for each move if it happens to concern—anyone else.'

'Other men?' She nodded and he smiled faintly, as if he understood exactly how Luis felt. 'That is to be expected, *chica*, if he loves you.'

'It's unbearable!' She had not meant to sound quite so emotional about it, and she shook her head slowly.

'I'm sorry, I don't mean to burden you with my personal problems, but you——'

'I encouraged you to talk.' A small tight smile admitted it. 'I hoped that talking about—whatever made you so troubled would help, Charlotte.' The black eyes searched slowly and intently over her small flushed face, and she shook his head. 'I do not like to see you look so unhappy.'

'It's not that I'm unhappy exactly,' she denied, wondering just how true it could be in time. 'But I can't go on living in the same house with people who distrust me.'

'So—you have decided to go home to England?' She nodded, wondering how she had managed to become so firmly committed to the idea without much effort. 'How soon will you be going?'

It came as a shock to her to realise how much it mattered that he had so coolly inquired how soon she intended leaving, instead of saying something to try and dissuade her. She did not want to go, she was quite sure of it when she looked across at him from the shadow of her lashes for a moment, she wanted to stay near him. It was silly and naïve of her to feel that way, for he would never even think of trying to change her mind, but she wished with all her heart that he would.

'I—I don't even know when,' she confessed, and laughed a little unsteadily, though there was no laughter in her eyes when she looked down at her hands. 'I haven't given it much thought yet, I only decided this morning.'

She glanced up in time to see an inquiring black brow. '*You* decided?'

'I—I felt it was the only solution after what hap-

170

pened. It can never be the same now, everything's changed.'

After a moment, he reached out and touched her, his hard strong fingers closing over hers, and when she looked up at him again there was a gentleness in his eyes that she had seen at other times, but that was all. 'And it is my fault, *pequeña*, I should have resisted the temptation to send a note with your hat when I returned it.'

'Oh, of course it isn't your fault! It's something that's been building up for some time. The fact that Luis found your note was just coincidence.' She looked down at her hands and the strong brown fingers that enclosed them, and felt a curious sense of loss suddenly. 'Luis wants to marry me, but I don't want to marry *him*.' Once more that shiveringly uncertain laugh fluttered from her throat, and she shook her head. 'It's a situation that can only be solved one way, Gerardo!'

'By you going home? Yes, I can see that.'

She wanted so desperately for him to ask her not to go, to express some form of regret at her going. Her heart was hammering hard at her ribs and she felt curiously light-headed as she sat there with her hands in his. It wasn't the effect of too much wine, she was certain of that, but the alternative that came to mind she hastily dismissed. She could not, she must not fall in love with him, and yet the longer she was with him, the more certain she became.

'If I may be allowed to offer my help.' His voice broke through the dizzying chaos of her thoughts, and it took a moment or two for the implication of what he was saying to dawn on her. 'If you would like to take advantage,' Gerardo went on, 'I have a plane flying to England next week, taking one of our executives to a conference in London—there will be plenty of room for you.'

Charlotte scarcely knew what to say. While she was trying her hardest not to fall in love with him, he was planning ways of helping her to fly home to England! Had it not been such a bitter pill for her to swallow, it would have been laughable.

Having lunch with Gerardo had been an unexpected treat, but Charlotte could do nothing about the sense of bitter disappointment she felt at his being so willing to speed her return home. Nothing was even settled as far as Martha was concerned, but Gerardo seemed to think that it was all cut and dried, and was anxious to help her on her way.

At her request he stopped the car at the gates of Casa Berganza instead of driving up to the house. There would be time enough, she thought, to say that she had had lunch with him without being seen arriving home in his car.

He came round to help her out of her seat, and the touch of his hand on her arm brought the inevitable response. She tried hard not to mind too much when he did no more than press his lips to her cheek for a moment when he said goodbye, but something in her stirred responses she seemed to have no control over.

'Gerardo!'

He was already half turned away when she called to him, and he turned back slowly, his expression hidden by the thick shadow of his lashes. '*Sí, pequeña?*'

Answering her in Spanish was unusual for him too, and she wondered vaguely if he had some idea of what she felt. He was experienced in the ways of women in love, and he probably knew exactly how she felt. Realising that made it much more difficult to know what to say, so that she could only stand there, listening to the insistent beat of her pulse for several seconds.

'I—I don't think I said thank you. For the offer of the flight home,' she added hastily.

'You will accept?'

Who could tell whether he wanted her to say she would or not? His dark features betrayed nothing at the moment, and yet it was the kind of face that could express so much if he chose to let it. The firm mouth showed neither impatience nor encouragement, and the look in his eyes was hidden from her. It was the thought of his perhaps finding her feeling for him an embarrassment that drove her to go on as she did.

'I don't know!' She laughed very unsteadily and searched his face once more with anxious blue eyes that hinted at defiance. 'Do you wish I *would*, Gerardo? Will you be glad not to have to worry about meeting me round every corner, or having me drop unconscious at your feet? Is that why you've offered to fly me home? Will you be glad to see the last of me, Gerardo?'

For a moment he said nothing and she had the awful suspicion that she had made the break between them, final and inevitable. But then he took a step towards her, and before she had time even to realise his intent, she was pulled hard against the vigorous warmth of his body and bound there with arms that threatened to crush the breath from her.

His mouth was on hers, fierce and hard, snatching her self-control from her with an irresistible force, and she closed her eyes as she clung to him, her body moulded like soft clay by the strength of his hands. Her heart was racing wildly when he released her, and

173

she gazed up at the stunning arrogance of his features with dazed eyes.

'Si, mi pichón, I want to see the last of you!' His voice caressed her like warm velvet, but it was firm too, so that she believed the words he said even while his breath fluttered against her mouth with each one of them. 'When you go, temptation goes with you, and I am growing tired of resisting!' Briefly again, his mouth took her soft, parted lips with an almost resentful fierceness, then he put her from him and turned away without another word.

CHAPTER NINE

CHARLOTTE was dazedly uncertain just what or how she felt. She had been so anxious for Gerardo to show some sign that he cared by asking her not to go, but his reaction to her provoking challenge, that he would be glad to see the last of her, had left her even more uncertain of how he really felt. She knew for certain, after those few cryptic words, that he found her a temptation, but why he wanted the temptation removed as soon as possible was even more confusing.

All that, and more, was going through her head while she walked through the tree-shaded garden to Casa Berganza. If she thought there was the slightest possiblity that Gerardo loved her, she would stay, no matter what she had to do to achieve it, but the discomfiting thought persisted that it was not love but something very much more earthy that he was so determined to resist.

As yet it had not occurred to her that she needed to settle with Martha when she would be actually leaving her employ. A week was such a short time in which to end a way of life that she had known for more than four months now, and enjoyed until very recently. Martha might not be willing to release her so soon, or she might even try to persuade her not to go at all; there were many things to take into account before she could accept Gerardo's offer to fly her home.

She looked at him in surprise when Luis came hurrying out into the hall almost before she stepped inside the house, and his expression of very evident relief at seeing her reproached her conscience so much that she hastily avoided his eyes. He came straight to her, reached out to take her hands, then thought better of it and used his own hands instead to lend emphasis to what he said.

'Oh, Charlotte, thank God!'

His fervour startled her momentarily, and she shook her head as she stood looking up at him. 'Luis, what's the matter?'

Martha had followed him out into the hall, and she too came over to her, her face serious but showing some of the same signs of relief as her son. Luis glanced over his shoulder at her, then frowned at Charlotte curiously.'*You* were the matter, Charlotte! You did not come down to lunch, and when Mamá went to your room to persuade you to join us, you were not there.'

It was not the moment to tell him that she had lunched with Gerardo instead, or even that she had seen him again, so she avoided the anxious enquiry in Martha's eyes and attempted to laugh off her temporary absence. 'Oh, I went for a walk—I needed to think things out.'

175

'For over three hours?'

He would have gone on, Charlotte thought, but his mother's warning hand on his arm stopped him and he looked round at her, then shrugged. Martha shook her head at him, and the small rueful smile she gave Charlotte puzzled her for a moment.

'You'd better come in to the *sala*, my dear, we have a great deal to talk about and this isn't really the best place for a serious conversation.'

A serious conversation implied only one thing, Charlotte thought, and followed Martha in to the *sala* with a whole new set of doubts crowding into her mind. She glanced at Luis, but he seemed almost deliberately to be avoiding her eyes. If only there had been some way to delay discussing her decision to leave until she felt more able to cope, she would have taken it, but at the moment she saw little option but to go where she was led.

In the big cool room that was now so touchingly familiar, they sat in three armchairs, carefully avoiding each other's eyes, as if there was something there that they preferred not to see. Luis was on edge and not quite so much in favour of the proposed conversation as Martha was, she guessed—his manner suggested that he was complying almost as unwillingly as she was herself.

'It's difficult to know how to begin,' Martha admitted. 'We—Luis and I—have so much to answer for, and it isn't easy to put into words.'

'To answer for?' Charlotte frowned at her curiously, wondering if she had guessed the right reason for the confrontation after all. A hasty glance at Luis's unresponsive face enlightened her no more. 'I don't quite understand, Aunt Martha.'

176

'How could you?' There was apology as well as uncertainty in Martha's expression and it was obvious that what she had to say did not come easily. 'Charlotte, Luis and I had a long talk after you left us this morning, and we both realised how—unfair we've been in the way we've acted towards you.'

'Oh, but, Aunt Martha——'

'Let me finish, dear, please.' She went on hastily, as if she feared she might lose track of what she had to say. 'It isn't easy, as I said, but I feel we must tell you now how wrong we've been to—to behave the way we have. Apologies are not easy, but we owe you our apologies for trying to—force the issue when you were unwilling. I mean regarding you and Luis, of course. I was too— insistent.'

It was at that point that Luis saw fit to take matters into his own hands. He got up from his chair and went to stand instead by the tall ornate fireplace, turned so that one arm lay along the mantel and he was looking down at them. There was a curious and half-defiant gleam in his dark eyes that endorsed her suspicion that he was less enthusiastic about this conversation than his mother was.

'What Mamá is trying to say, Charlotte, is that I have taken too much for granted these past weeks, in assuming that you felt as deeply for me as I do for you, and in doing so I have perhaps——' His shrug was a small helpless gesture that she found infinitely touching. 'I have caused you unhappiness, Charlotte, when my intention was exactly the opposite—I am sorry.'

'I was as much to blame,' Martha insisted, unwilling to see him take the full blame on himself. 'I had no right to expect Charlotte to order her life to suit my plans, regardless of her own feelings. She insisted that she was not—as fond of you as I hoped, and I simply refused to believe it.' Her smile did not reach her eyes, and Charlotte realised just how hard it was for her to speak as she did with her son there to hear. 'My pride wouldn't let me believe there was a young woman alive who could resist my son.'

Charlotte, to her dismay, found herself close to tears, and she held her hands tightly together on her lap while she tried to steady her voice. 'Please—neither of you has anything to apologise for. Aunt Martha, I know—I think I know how much you wanted me to——' A glance at Luis's face made it impossible for her to go on, and she shook her head. 'No one has to apologise for anything—I've been very happy here.'

'But you will still leave us?' It was Luis's quiet resigned voice that asked the inevitable question, and she took a second to answer him.

Looking down at her hands, she nodded. 'Yes, Luis. I—I feel I have to go, it would be better if I did.'

'Because you do not trust me to keep my word?'

'Oh no, no—it's not that at all.'

'I promise there would be no pressure on you to—do as we want you to. We would not try to run your life for you as we have perhaps attempted to do—I promise you that, Charlotte, so will you not stay?'

It was the moment she had been dreading, and Charlotte would have liked more time to prepare herself for this final decision. If she stayed, how could she avoid seeing Gerardo? And each time she saw him now, she would fall more deeply in love with him, she knew. Even if she never saw him again she would be aware of him there, so close and yet so unattainable in that huge, glowering castle. In time he might perhaps find himself a suitable bride, a Spanish bride, to share his castle with him.

The latter idea she quickly dismissed from her mind, and she glanced at Martha, wondering if she would eventually guess her real reason for her need to go. 'I —I can't stay, Luis.' She shook her head firmly, as much to deny herself any flutter of hope, as to deny him. 'I have to—to get away—I really have to!'

Luis said nothing, he simply looked at her for a second or two then shrugged slowly, as if he could think of nothing more to persuade her. '*Así sea*,' he said, and reached for a cheroot from the box on the mantel, with hands that shook with emotion.

The expression on Martha's face was enough to tell her that she had a suspicion at least of why it was so imperative for her to go as far away from San Cristóbal as possible. 'I'm sorry,' she said, and Charlotte believed she meant it kindly.

The need to cry was beginning to become urgent, and yet she was reluctant to give way to tears until she could do so in the privacy of her own room. 'I—I wondered how long you wanted me to stay,' she ventured in a small shaky voice, and Martha looked vaguely taken aback for a moment.

'Why, I haven't really thought about it, my dear.'

'I'd like to go quite soon, if that's possible, perhaps next week. I have the opportunity of a seat on an aircraft, and I—I thought——'

Martha was staring at her, so was Luis, and with the old familiar frown of suspicion drawing his brows together. 'Next week? So soon? Why so soon, Charlotte?'

Her hands were pressed so tightly together that the bones of her knuckles showed white under the skin, and she tried hard to keep her voice steady. 'I—I saw

Gerardo while I was out,' she said, and did not even notice the familiar use of his christian name, although she glanced briefly at Luis when she heard him catch his breath. 'I was such a long time gone because he—he gave me lunch.'

'*Caramba!*' Luis swore under his breath, and she realised hazily that it would never have been possible for him to behave with as much restraint as he had promised. 'You have been to the castle again?'

'No, we—we drove into Arcos.'

'While we were worrying where you were!'

She looked at him, trying not to let him see the anger and resentment she felt at his reproof—how could he possibly understand how she felt? 'I had no reason to suppose I would even be missed, Luis.' Her voice was shaky but she went on determinedly. 'I didn't go out with any intention of meeting Gerardo, if that's what you're thinking, but when I saw him and he asked me to have lunch with him—well, I saw no reason not to.'

Luis swore again, and with such vehemence that even Martha frowned at him. 'Luis, we've made a promise! There's to be no more interference in Charlotte's affairs, we agreed on that. We don't have the right to pass an opinion on whether or not she should have had lunch with Don Gerardo—it doesn't concern us.'

For a moment it looked as if Luis was going to defy her opinion and dismiss the promise he had made as impossible to keep. Instead, after a second or two, he spread his hands in a curiously touching gesture of resignation and looked at Charlotte ruefully. 'Will you forgive me, yet again, Charlotte? It is simply that I cannot be uninterested in whatever you do—I am sorry, I will try not to let it happen again.'

Charlotte said nothing, only smiled a little vaguely at him, before giving her attention once more to Martha. 'I would have told you about it, Aunt Martha, only I—I wanted time to think first.'

'Yes, of course you did!'

If only she had not seen that kindly look of understanding in Martha's eyes, she thought, it would have made it so much easier to explain. As it was, knowing that Martha had a very good idea by now of what the trouble was made her not only more inhibited but also more tearful. She felt a lump in her throat that was harder to swallow than ever before, and tears prickled her eyes, almost too close to be held back.

'Was it this—meeting with Don Gerardo that decided you to go home so soon?' Martha asked, and Charlotte nodded silently. 'I see.'

'Oh, but I don't think you do, quite!' Charlotte denied in a voice that quavered somewhere between crying and laughing hysterically. 'You see, Gerardo's so anxious to be rid of me that he's offered to let me fly home in his own plane—next week!'

'Oh, Charlotte, my dear!'

Charlotte waited to hear no more. She got to her feet, suddenly clumsy and blinded by tears that rolled down her cheeks as she headed for the door. The die was cast and she had nothing more to hide—her tears and those last bitter words must have made it as clear to Luis as it was to his mother just how she felt about Gerardo Cortez—and just how little chance there was for her.

It seemed imperative somehow to let Gerardo know as soon as possible that she would be accepting his offer to fly her home, and Charlotte thought about it to the

181

exclusion of practically everything else all the next day. It seemed important to let him know that she intended going out of his life for ever, but it proved rather less simple to do than she anticipated.

In a moment of bravado she dialled his number on the telephone and asked the efficient Miss Fane if she might speak with him. Whether or not he really was out at the time, she could not prove, but she had little option in the circumstances but to accept it as a fact, and it was the possibility of being turned away by that same diligent watch-dog that deterred her at first from going to the castle to see him.

Remembering how Miss Fane's efforts to prevent her seeing him had failed last time encouraged her, and eventually she made up her mind. She told Martha of her intention, but said nothing to Luis, and without a doubt Martha would have been sternly against any such rashness in former circumstances—now she merely shook her head in despair at the way things had turned out, and implied that she understood her reasons.

On foot, because she felt it was incongruous to arrive on a visit to a castle riding a bicycle, she walked down the hot dusty road to the village. San Cristóbal was so endearingly familiar to her now that she felt tears in her eyes at the thought of leaving it, and she shook her head impatiently as she neared the last bend into the village proper, pushing the little white hat more firmly on to her head. It was too late now to become morbid—the pleasant dream of San Cristóbal was over and she was on her way to see the man who had ended it for her.

In England she would have been observing the rule of the road, and walking facing the oncoming traffic, but there was virtually no traffic through San Cristóbal, so she stayed in the shadow of the grove of olives whose shade edged the road right down to the edge of the village.

A car horn blaring noisily on the hot still air had her jumping for safety to the very border of the trees as the car swung out around her in a cloud of dust. It was big and black and the driver was already out of his seat and striding back towards her, even before she had time to recover her breath.

Black eyes glowed like polished jet in the dark arrogance of his features, and he stood in silence, looking down at her, almost as if he had never seen her before. 'Are you so determined to make me run you down, *mi querida?*' he asked, and his voice was shaky with emotion, although she could scarcely believe it.

She raised her eyes only as far as the half-mocking but infinitely disturbing smile on his mouth. 'I—I was on my way to see you.' Heaven knew why she had to come out with it so impulsively, but her legs seemed barely capable of holding her quite suddenly, and her voice had a small and breathless sound as she coped with the urgent beat of her heart.

'So?' He did not touch her, and yet she felt as shiveringly aware of that lean vigorous body as if she was pressed close to it. His hands were at his sides, but the long brown fingers were curled slightly, as if he held himself in check. 'I have been expecting you before this,' he told her.

His exact meaning eluded her, but she assumed he referred to the fact that she had not yet accepted his offer to fly her home, and in the circumstances his haste to know her decision hurt more than he could possibly know.

'I did try to contact you. I—I rang yesterday, but your—Miss Fane told me that you were out.'

'So María told me.'

She did not quite understand that, but she was rather too confused at the moment to understand anything, and she looked up briefly, into his eyes. 'I didn't have the nerve to try again,' she confessed, and caught her breath when the familiar deep softness of his laughter shivered along her spine.

'I have to believe that, *mi pichón*! Señorita Fane is what you call a female dragon, I believe.'

It occurred to Charlotte suddenly that that was the second very intimate endearment he had used, and she overlooked his opinion of his secretary while she tried to gather her thoughts.

'I—I didn't know if your secretary would let me in if I called, but——'

'Very probably she would not have done,' Gerardo told her coolly. 'Just as she informed you that I was not at home yesterday when you telephoned.' The black eyes gleamed darkly below straight dark brows and for a second he looked every inch the autocrat. 'That is why she is now under notice.'

Almost too stunned to accept the full implication of what he said, Charlotte shook her head slowly as she stared at him with her lips parted in surprise. 'She's—leaving?'

'She has been given little option,' Gerardo informed her, and for a second she once more caught a glimpse of that suggestion of cruelty in the straightness of his mouth.

She was confused, more confused than ever she had been, and she tried to bring herself back to the reason she had been on her way to see him. 'I thought it might be easier if I called at the castle, I wanted to get in touch with you, and——'

A large but infinitely gentle hand touched her cheek lightly then moved around under her silky hair to the nape of her neck. 'You have only to reach out to be in touch, *querida*.'

Looking up at him with appealing blue eyes that still held the mistiness of recent tears, she searched that dark proud face for guidance. 'Gerardo, you—you said——'

'I said that I was tired of resisting, did I not?' She nodded, and the white hat slipped a little further to the back of her head. 'So—I have decided to resist no more, *mi pequeña*! Since you have not been to see me, I was on my way to see you, whether or not it was discreet in view of Luis Berganza's jealousy!'

'You were on your way to see me?'

'*Si, mi querida.*' His other hand slid beneath her hair and his fingers cradled her head, two hard warm palms either side of her neck while he looked down at her with an intensity that burned her like a flame. 'Do I presume too much when I hope that you love me, *mi* Carlota? Do you really wish me to send you back to England on that plane, or will you stay here—with me?'

'Oh yes, yes, I don't *want* to go!'

She no longer even realised that they were standing on the dusty road into San Cristóbal. They could have been in the middle of a busy street in some town and she would not have either known or cared. The olive trees shaded them from the worst of the sun's heat and somewhere below in the village, the melodious bell in the convent of San Cristóbal chimed a call to prayer.

It was all so right suddenly, so peaceful and yet so exciting.

'*Te quiero, amada.*' His voice, velvet soft, caressed her like the gentle hands on her neck. 'I love you, Charlotte, I cannot hide it any longer, nor can I deny myself the exquisite pleasure of your love.'

For a moment she looked up into his face. Into the depthless black glow of his eyes and the exciting strength of his features, then she buried her face against him and his arms drew her close. Her body trembled like a leaf as he held her, his hands gently persuasive, as his head bent to touch his mouth to hers.

'Oh, Gerardo, Gerardo, I was so afraid you wanted me to go!'

He said nothing, but for a second only the black eyes burned like coals between their thick short lashes, then he took her mouth again with a fierceness that deprived her of breath and will-power and transported her swiftly into another world where nothing was impossible. The lean, hard warmth of his body and the unyielding fierceness of his arms possessed her, and she offered no resistance.

It seemed like an eternity before he released her mouth and looked down at her, and yet the bell was still chiming in the background, and there was still no sign of another soul on that steep dusty road into the village. She looked up at him for a long time, her hands either side of his head, stroking the thick black hair, then she shook her head slowly.

'I love you,' she said in a small and shakily unsteady voice. 'I was so unhappy when I left the house to come and see you, and now I——' She laughed and her blue eyes shone like jewels in the pale golden shadow of her face. 'Why did you want to resist falling in love, Gerardo? Why, my darling?'

He took so long to answer that she wondered if his reason was a painful one—if he had loved before and— She hastily shook her head, and smiled up at him, and he kissed her mouth in a way that made her forget even the question she had asked him.

'You are—different, *mi querida*.' A sober look gave his dark features sternness for a moment and she pressed closer to him when it seemed he was lost to her for a second. 'There were many women, Charlotte, you know about that—Martha Berganza will have told you, I think, if not her son!'

'I know.' She tiptoed and kissed his mouth. 'I know about your mother too—as you say, Martha told me, but only when I asked about you.' A fleeting smile admitted her curiosity. 'I was interested enough to ask, even then.'

His arms tightened and he looked down at her with a fierce black glow in his eyes that shivered through her. 'I had never known anyone like you before, and I was—wary.' It was hard to believe, but somehow she had to believe it, even though she shook her head. 'I started to fall in love with you, and there seemed nothing I could do to stop myself, until in the end I felt I must send you away on that plane or I was bound to betray how I felt.'

'And now you have!'

He held her close, his eyes warm and exciting as a caress, his hands moulding her close to him. 'I did not believe myself capable of being a good husband to someone like you, *mi pequeña*, but now——'

'Now?' Charlotte prompted gently, and he shook his head firmly.

'Now I am sure that I will be, *mi amante*, if you will have me!'

'Did you ever doubt that I would?' Charlotte asked softly, and lifted her face to him again.

Did you miss any of these exciting Harlequin Omnibus 3-in-1 volumes?

Each volume contains 3 great novels by one author for only $1.95.
See order coupon.

Violet Winspear #3
The Cazalet Bride (#1434)
Beloved Castaway (#1472)
The Castle of the Seven Lilacs (#1514)

Anne Mather
Charlotte's Hurricane (#1487)
Lord of Zaracus (#1574)
The Reluctant Governess (#1600)

Anne Hampson

Anne Hampson #1
Unwary Heart (#1388)
Precious Waif (#1420)
The Autocrat of Melhurst (#1442)

Betty Neels
Tempestuous April (#1441)
Damsel in Green (#1465)
Tulips for Augusta (#1529)

Essie Summers #3
Summer in December (#1416)
The Bay of the Nightingales (#1445)
Return to Dragonshill (#1502)

Margaret Way

Margaret Way
King Country (#1470)
Blaze of Silk (#1500)
The Man from Bahl Bahla (#1530)

---

40 magnificent Omnibus volumes to choose from:

Essie Summers #1
Bride in Flight (#933)
Postscript to Yesterday (#1119)
Meet on My Ground (#1326)

Jean S. MacLeod
The Wolf of Heimra (#990)
Summer Island (#1314)
Slave of the Wind (#1339)

Eleanor Farnes
The Red Cliffs (#1335)
The Flight of the Swan (#1280)
Sister of the Housemaster (#975)

Susan Barrie #1
Marry a Stranger (#1034)
Rose in the Bud (#1168)
The Marriage Wheel (#1311)

Violet Winspear #1
Beloved Tyrant (#1032)
Court of the Veils (#1267)
Palace of the Peacocks (#1318)

Isobel Chace
The Saffron Sky (#1250)
A Handful of Silver (#1306)
The Damask Rose (#1334)

Joyce Dingwell #1
Will You Surrender (#1179)
A Taste for Love (#1229)
The Feel of Silk (#1342)

Sara Seale
Queen of Hearts (#1324)
Penny Plain (#1197)
Green Girl (#1045)

Jane Arbor
A Girl Named Smith (#1000)
Kingfisher Tide (#950)
The Cypress Garden (#1336)

Anne Weale
The Sea Waif (#1123)
The Feast of Sara (#1007)
Doctor in Malaya (#914)

Essie Summers #2
His Serene Miss Smith (#1093)
The Master to Tawhai (#910)
A Place Called Paradise (#1156)

Catherine Airlie
Doctor Overboard (#979)
Nobody's Child (#1258)
A Wind Sighing (#1328)

Violet Winspear #2
Bride's Dilemma (#1008)
Tender Is the Tyrant (#1208)
The Dangerous Delight (#1344)

Kathryn Blair
Doctor Westland (#954)
Battle of Love (#1038)
Flowering Wilderness (#1148)

Rosalind Brett
The Girl at White Drift (#1101)
Winds of Enchantment (#1176)
Brittle Bondage (#1319)

Rose Burghley
Man of Destiny (#960)
The Sweet Surrender (#1023)
The Bay of Moonlight (#1245)

Iris Danbury
Rendezvous in Lisbon (#1178)
Doctor at Villa Ronda (#1257)
Hotel Belvedere (#1331)

Amanda Doyle
A Change for Clancy (#1085)
Play the Tune Softly (#1116)
A Mist in Glen Torran (#1308)

Great value in Reading!
Use the handy order form

Elizabeth Hoy
Snare the Wild Heart
(#992)
The Faithless One
(#1104)
Be More than Dreams
(#1286)

Roumelia Lane
House of the Winds
(#1262)
A Summer to Love
(#1280)
Sea of Zanj (#1338)

Margaret Malcolm
The Master of
Normanhurst (#1028)
The Man in Homespun
(#1140)
Meadowsweet (#1164)

Joyce Dingwell #2
The Timber Man (#917)
Project Sweetheart
(#964)
Greenfingers Farm
(#999)

Marjorie Norell
Nurse Madeline of Eden
Grove (#962)
Thank You, Nurse
Conway (#1097)
The Marriage of Doctor
Royle (#1177)

Anne Durham
New Doctor at
Northmoor (#1242)
Nurse Sally's Last
Chance (#1281)
Mann of the Medical
Wing (#1313)

Henrietta Reid
Reluctant Masquerade
(#1380)
Hunter's Moon (#1430)
The Black Delaney
(#1460)

Lucy Gillen
The Silver Fishes
(#1408)
Heir to Glen Ghyll
(#1450)
The Girl at Smuggler's
Rest (#1533)

Anne Hampson #2
When the Bough Breaks
(#1491)
Love Hath an Island
(#1522)
Stars of Spring (#1551)

Essie Summers #4
No Legacy for Lindsay
(#957)
No Orchids by Request
(#982)
Sweet Are the Ways
(#1015)

Mary Burchell #3
The Other Linding Girl
(#1431)
Girl with a Challenge
(#1455)
My Sister Celia (#1474)

Susan Barrie #2
Return to Tremarth
(#1359)
Night of the Singing
Birds (#1428)
Bride in Waiting
(#1526)

Violet Winspear #4
Desert Doctor (#921)
The Viking Stranger
(#1080)
The Tower of the Captive
(#1111)

Essie Summers #5
Heir to Windrush Hill
(#1055)
Rosalind Comes Home
(#1283)
Revolt — and Virginia
(#1348)

Doris E. Smith
To Sing Me Home
(#1427)
Seven of Magpies
(#1454)
Dear Deceiver (#1599)

Katrina Britt
Healer of Hearts
(#1393)
The Fabulous Island
(#1490)
A Spray of Edelweiss
(#1626)

Betty Neels #2
Sister Peters in
Amsterdam (#1361)
Nurse in Holland
(#1385)
Blow Hot — Blow Cold
(#1409)

Amanda Doyle #2
The Girl for Gillgong
(#1351)
The Year at Yattabilla
(#1448)
Kookaburra Dawn
(#1562)

Complete and mail this coupon today!